Heroes of Levea

Heroes of Levea

© 2018 by Rebecca Smith

ISBN: 9781798941607

Dedication

To my Creator and my family

Acknowledgments

I WOULD LIKE to acknowledge my Creator for giving me the ideas in this book and the ability to carry them out. May He get the glory!

I want to thank my mom for her support and fanfare.

I want to thank my dad for his support and critical eye.

I would like to thank my brother for being a friend I can trust to keep the ideas I have for books a secret.

I could have never been able to publish my book without the guidance and advice from my editor, Mrs. Linda Stubblefield. And I must credit my amazing book cover and the art in the text to Mrs. Claire Fulton.

Thank you, everybody!

About the Author

REBECCA LOIS LILLIAN Smith is a missionary kid living on the island of Barbados in the West Indies who has spent four years writing and one year of refining *Heroes of Levea*. She works with her family in the church they started, the St. Philip Independent Baptist Church. Becca teaches the girls Sunday school class and works in their junior church and their Kids-In-Training club on Sunday night. She enjoys writing, painting, and reading.

Characters

HE ROYAL CLANS

Royal Clan Ilindel
    King Rigal and Queen Aan Ilindel
      Princess Kanea Ilindel

Royal Clan Opalestene
    King Andres Opalestene

Royal Clan Werytil
    King Fwerdin Werytil
      Prince Dashel Werytil

Royal Clan Videan
    King Zictor Videan

Royal Clan San
    King Trea San

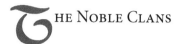

The Noble Clans

Noble Clan Salindone
Lord Nanook and Lady Nan Salindone
Lordlings Nicoron and Asher Salindone

Noble Clan Quariopel
Lordling Denel Quariopel

Noble Clan Helyanwe
Duke Runtron and Duchess Reen Helyanwe
Dukelings Kaete, Lura, and Tari Helyanwe

Noble Clan Colodrung
Master Colodrung
Masterlings Aster, Astar, and Astair Colodrung

Noble Clan Uytil
Lordling Ghagden Uytil

The Warrior Class

Tanyon Fitherlew, *trainer of warriors*
Jakkon Kingerly, *sentry*
Burladase, *captain*

The Servant Class

Tif, *personal assistant to Dukeling Tari*

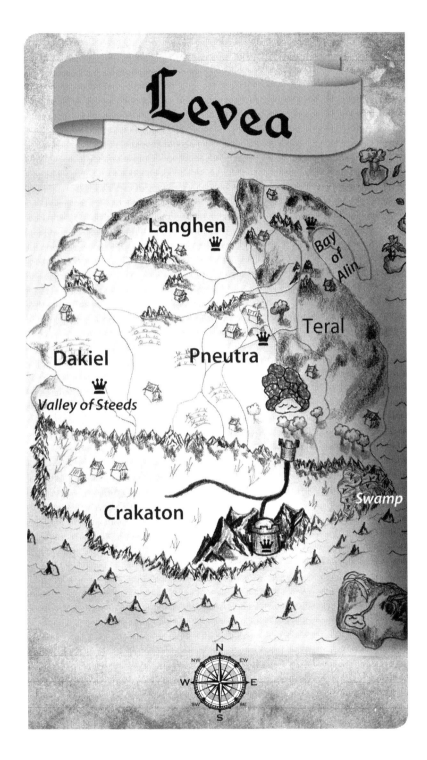

Map Legend

THE HUTS REPRESENT villages. One hut per village except for Crakaton where three huts represent one village.

The crowns signify the citadels or capital cities.

The triangles on land represent mountain ranges. The triangles in the ocean south of Crakaton represent sea stacks.

Farmlands are signified by rows of crops.

The thin lines in Crakaton represent the tall grass described in the book.

The humps northwest of Pneutra and southeast of Dakiel represent hills.

Just south of the Pneutraite citadel is the woodland arena.

The islands to the north and east of Teral compose part of the Teralian Archipelago.

Introduction

IN ANCIENT TIMES, a giant island in the middle of a vast sea was named Levea by its possessors. Sailors of an unknown origin from across the ocean had sailed to Levea and inhabited the island. Where these travelers came from is likely to remain a secret until the end of time. These possessors found different sections of land that suited them well and claimed the acreage for their own. In time five cantons named Langhen, Dakiel, Pneutra, Teral, and Crakaton were established. Each canton was ruled independently with its own resources from which to draw wealth.

In the northwest, Langhen was composed primarily of highlands and mountains with few forests or farmland and absolutely no beaches. Langhen could perhaps boast the title "Richest Canton," for its mountains were filled with coal and precious substances. Jewels were in great demand for the pompous royalty and nobility; gold had become somewhat of a money standard. Iron was another abundant resource in the mountains, but Langhen's iron was not just any iron. Known as feather iron, the lightweight, sturdy metal could be crafted to create the best armor on the face of Levea. Langhen could also boast of its exceptionally expert warriors. The hulking men comprising the army of Langhen led by the fearless counts struck fear into the hearts of their enemies.

Dakiel, which was located directly south of Langhen, mainly consisted of the valley between Langhen and the fault-block elevations of Crakaton. The soil was very fertile, and farming was the main industry of the canton. However, the pride and joy of Dakiel rested in their equine inhabitants. Powerful, spirited horses pounded the plains of Dakiel. Horsemen tamed and trained these spirited animals and created a powerful cavalry led by the masters of Dakiel.

Pneutra, the heart of Levea, was filled with healthy forests. Lumber became the main income for many Pneutraites, as well as hunting. With forests came wild game, and the choicest wild game took refuge in the midst of Pneutra. Consequently, archery became a popular sport. The lords of Pneutra unilaterally claimed the unerring aim of their warriors could not be bested by anyone in the land.

To the northeast was Teral, the smallest canton in area, but not in industries. Around the beaches of Teral lay the Teralian Archipelago, the richest fishing territory in Levea. Sailing merchants received strange and wonderful trinkets when visiting the Teralian territory. Their glass and jewel sculptures were impressive, and the coconuts gathered in demand by other seaports in Levea. Sailing was the largest and most compelling sport in the Bay of Alin. Of course, Teralian dukes captained the best navy in Teral.

Crakaton, oh Crakaton—the vastest canton in Levea—covered the entire south. The unknown terrain was surrounded by fault-block mountains that reached the sky. The only way inside of the land was through a narrow pass that connected the canton with Pneutra. In ancient times, a foreign people had come and flooded the canton, blocking the pass with an impregnable fort. King Trea San, their ruthless tyrant, was greedy for power and had launched an all-out attack on all of Levea. The fierce and ruthless Crakatonian warriors used every dirty trick imaginable, but the odds were against them. The tyrant and his army was eventually driven back into his fort and never seen again. After a few hundred years, people forgot about the king and left the forsaken land to itself.

Peace and prosperity swept through the rest of the land. The citizens were happy and full, pleased with their monarchs, and soon the cantons became dependent on each other. International trade became important for the thriving of each canton. Except for a few skirmishes that were easily reconcilable, the island hosted no wars or battles. Each day seemed like an everlasting morning filled with security and prosperity, but in truth, every good thing must come to an end.

Prologue

THE POUNDING OF horses' hooves was exhilarating! What better way to relax than a stag hunt in March! Hunt a stag all day and sing around a campfire at night. King Rigal of Pneutra needed this relaxing time away from the citadel and away from the pressures of kingly life. His noble stallion led in the chase, and the pure white mane waved majestically in the breeze.

"You're a devious one!" The king admiringly shouted at his quarry as the buck suddenly changed his course of direction. Hounds bayed after the deer, and a falcon whistled. Their hunt had become full-blown!

A sharp yip sounded from one of the hunting dogs.

Suddenly the king's mount snorted and reared. "Steady, Malifast!" With a strong hand, Rigal settled the steed. "What ails you enough to interrupt our stag hunt?"

Malifast's ears began flicking back and forth, and the horse continued to stomp restlessly. Suddenly, the horse trumpeted wildly, tossed his head, and stamped his feet.

A vibrating growl echoed from deep from within the nearby forest. Rigal stood in his stirrups. "That doesn't sound like one of our hounds," he muttered to no one in particular.

The same chilling growl suddenly sounded from directly behind him. The king quickly turned Malifast to find himself facing an enormous monster. Rigal drew his sword and yelled for help, but his shout of alarm did him no good.

Chapter One

THE CRISP, EARLY fall wind whipped his dark-brown hair, making his hazel eyes water. His lanky and slightly muscular form shivered, and he wished he had a coat or cloth to shield himself from the chilly breeze. The youth of seventeen years strolled in the courtyard of his family's estate. His name was Nicoron Salindone, known informally as Nic, the eldest son of Lord Nanook, a predominant noble in the canton of Pneutra.

Nicoron was a guard of the Queen Aan and her fair daughter Kanea, and his pay was the opportunity of becoming a lord, a noble. He looked forward to the day when Queen Aan would make him a lord with the accompanying huge ceremony and fancy suits. Many officials would be present to see another one of their youth become a man.

"First I must earn the honor." He reminded himself that before a nobling could become a lord, he must do something worthy of the position. Nic did not worry though. He flexed his biceps, and confidence filled his soul.

At the time, Nic and his partner, another lordling, were on vacation. This time was used to prepare for upcoming games for the young nobility. They trained in their free hours back at the citadel, but nothing could replace the three-week warm up they had to their advantage.

A call sounded from the house, disturbing the youth's thought. The call he heard was one no young person would ever miss—the dinner bell.

~

Meanwhile, in the citadel of Pneutra, Princess Kanea Ilindel gazed out of her bedroom window, as if in the strongest trance ever. The princess was a mere sixteen and had hair the color of the dusk sky; her eyes were a color akin to the forest. She was taller than other girls her age, by a few centimeters, and was rather a thin sort.

Usually Kanea was like the sun, shining with a smile wide and bright, but like the sun, there were times when her smile faded like afternoon—dusk to night. Night was ruling now, the darkest night in the life of this princess.

The darkness of this night had been caused by the death of her beloved father. The funeral was exactly a month before, and following that was the three-day, worldwide mourning. For the three days following the funeral, lanterns were lit not to go out until the vigil was complete. At least one window of every household and citadel held a lighted lantern in remembrance of the king who had died.

King Rigal was a man of honor, valor, and character. Many kings would have been greedy and would have sought to cheat their subjects out of their livings, but not Rigal. He set a fair tax, not outrageous nor varying from noble to peasant. Oh, how Kanea missed the tall figure of her father!

The princess fingered her pendant, an heirloom her father had given her when she was thirteen.

"Protect it, Kanea; care for it," he had told her when he had presented the heirloom to her.

"Is it really that old?" she had asked as she examined it.

"The pendant is very old, but it is also the most important item you will possess in your youth."

Kanea did not know what her father meant, but she did protect it and wore it all the time. As memories flooded her mind, tears filled her eyes, threatening to spill over.

Nicoron arrived at the family dining table.

"How was the day, son?" inquired his father.

"Fine, the courtyard looks outstanding." Then addressing his mother, he asked, "What have you been doing while I was away?"

Nan smiled at her eldest. "Oh, not much. Then Asher gave me the idea of tulips for the spring." Asher was Nicoron's fourteen-year-old brother. He smirked. In his eyes, his family was just fine. Though the sadness of losing their king encircled their souls, the love that bonded them together warmed their hearts. Asher did not show his grief, but Nic knew that he was grieving as much as anyone else. Nic's thoughts were interrupted by his father's addressing him.

"Nicoron, look at this." Nic picked up a letter his father set before him. The front was white with the king of Pneutra's seal on it. He opened it to see an invitation in elegant writing to the Nobling Duels. His heart raced.

The Nobling Duels were a way for every nobling in Levea to test their skills against each other. Fighting and survival were the two main categories with many competitions under each division. Every nobling was invited to enter some sort of game. His invitation cleared him for a fencing team sport and hunting. Nic was slightly disappointed at the latter because archery was not his best skill, nonetheless it was a part of hunting. Asher received a similar invitation.

"I get to enter my horse in the jumping competition this year, and I'm doing archery!" Asher was the archer and horseman in the family. Nic told them what he was doing.

"Who are you going to choose to be your partner?" Nan asked when she heard of the fencing team. Nicoron could think of no one better than his best friend and fellow guard, Denel Quariopel.

～

The evening meal was silent, the only sound being the soft music of lutes and pipes that would lullaby any child. Kanea moved her salted fish around the majestic plate with her fork, not at all enticed by the delectable scent and the palatable dainties. Queen Aan sat at the head of the table just as silent as her daughter. Her eyes were red from weeping, and every so often a desolate tear escaped to linger. Midnight was darker every moment as the kingdom mourned the loss of their beloved king. King Rigal of Pneutra had been slain by a creature so horrific no one dared to describe it. Kanea was now terrified to walk outside the royal court let alone in the forest.

～

In the next country, a fourteen-year-old nobling of Teral swung her legs over a balcony. Auburn, curly hair was pulled back with a ribbon, and hazel eyes scanned the horizon for any remaining glimpses of the ocean.

"Those palms keep disturbing my view," Tari Helyanwe, the daughter of the Duke Runtron and Duchess Reen, grumbled in frustration. A white cat with fluffy fur that reminded Tari of whitecaps along the seashore, sat next to the girl. Yoko meowed in reply and gazed at Tari with ocean-blue eyes. Tari's personal assistant, Tif, came onto the balcony.

"Lovely night isn't it, Dukeling Tari?" she asked as she took in the salty smell of the evening breeze.

"Yes, it is," Tari replied shortly. Silence momentarily filled the room.

Tif sighed and stated, "Time for supper. Are you ready?"

"Yes, indeed!" Tari exclaimed. "I'm famished." She smoothed her pleated aqua dress, then raced downstairs. In the dining hall the dukeling saw her parents and her other two older sisters, Kaete and Lura. Tari quickly took her place at the end and greeted everyone. Dinner continued as normal with discussion of hunts, rides and boating in the bay. The whole family was athletic and eager for any adventure; the dining room was full of proof for that fact. Trophies won in races, paintings of sailing ships from past generations, bows and swords adorned the walls of the room.

Tari dreamed of winning races with her black steed Prince. He was a powerful horse with the speed of a falcon, and Tari was sure they could win races together. Tari had an unusual hunger for adventure and danger. Always did she wish that something superbly exciting would happen. Duke Runtron revealed three envelopes from underneath the table that possessed the seal of their king. He smiled and asked his girls if they knew what it was. The trio replied simultaneously.

"Invitations to the Nobling Duels!"

"You are…" He stopped for the sake of suspense. "Correct!" As they cheered, he passed them their invitations.

"I get to participate in archery." Kaete squealed in delight.

"I'm invited to the horse jumping competition," Tari announced excitedly.

"Well, I'm entered in the eating game!" Lura exclaimed. The others looked at her with strange looks. "Just kidding! I get archery too, and the—"

"Cross-country relay race!" the girls chorused. They tucked their letters underneath their plates.

"Finally, some diversion," Lura exclaimed.

"As if we haven't had fun in the past?" Semi-sophisticated Kaete inquired in a scolding manner. Tari replied with a wink.

"With *you* around, who can have fun?" her eldest sister rolled her eyes.

"Just so you know…I'm just as excited as you are about the Nobling Duels!" The nineteen-year-old sniffed, and Lura smiled.

"We know, Kaete. But you're just so much fun to tease— even though you don't bite," she ended playfully.

Their mother laughed at their chatter. "Girls, I am sure that we all will have an enjoyable time," she assured them.

"So when do we set off?" Tari asked, and her father answered.

"In the morning. We have the horses rested for the journey and the necessities for camping on the way." The trio shouted when camping was mentioned, for they all loved living simply in the wilderness for a few a days.

"Just a few more trophies for our trophy case," Kaete added with a toss of her head.

"Noblings from all over Levea will be competing," Lura reminded her elder sister that they were not the only ones who had been invited to the competition.

"So?" Tari countered. "That has never stopped us yet."

Nicoron raised his sword and swung it to block the oncoming sword.

"You know, Nicoron, we are dueling—not really fighting." Denel told his sparring partner.

"Denel, if we will be a team in the Nobling Duels, we need to try to sharpen our skills."

"As if we haven't been training since last year," the lordling replied. "Why are you so intense on training?"

"I simply desire to bring honor on my name."

"And a title no doubt."

"You can read me too well."

"That is not hard. Also, I bet you would enjoy the attention of some ladies as well," Denel replied with a raised brow.

Nicoron threw his arms wide open. "What am I? A book?"

"Now you've got it." Denel smiled and put a hand on his

friend's shoulder. "You just need to watch out, friend. Your desires may turn around and bite you. Not all girls are nice."

The lordling nodded. "I know, friend. I will be careful."

"And now…" Denel paused to raise his sword. "Prepare to be defeated."

Nicoron followed the gesture. "Right back at you."

Chapter Two

REPARATION FOR THE Nobling Duels kept Pneutra busy, and Kanea had no time to dwell on the passing of her father. She had to keep checking on the servants to certify that the noblings' guest rooms would be in perfect order for their arrival. As princess, she also had the responsibility of making the guests feel at home. She assigned well-trained and private servants to each of the guests and also worried about the decor of the rooms. Needlessly perhaps, but the welcoming nature of the young princess obliged her to order the decoration of the rooms indigenous to the guest's home canton. Sometimes she wished that the various cantons could rotate the responsibility of the duels. However, Pneutra's predominantly central location on the island placed this canton in the ideal position to host the duels and thus had been chosen as the permanent house of the Nobling duels.

Kanea's thoughts were interrupted by a servant's asking her opinion on one of the guest rooms decor. The room was to be inhabited by the dukelings. The princess gazed around the room with pleasure. The wall was painted a light-blue with discreet curves of darker blues and aqua blues forming a wavy pattern. A painting of Teral's royal navy was portrayed in a unique frame on the wall. White sand and seashells from Teral's beaches had been glued to the frame.

"Perfection," Kanea breathed.

∽

"Is a fifteen-minute waxing really all that necessary, Nic?" Asher asked after watching his brother's meticulous sword care.

"If you want to use your sword to its full abilities, then yes," Nicoron replied with a nod. "And I want my sword capable of its full abilities." He imagined a trophy or medal he could win for some sort of contest displayed in their family trophy case. How proud he would make his parents if he won a game! Neither he nor Asher were of those who won something every year.

"I just know I will bring something home this year," Asher interrupted Nicoron with his determined statement.

The elder smiled. "I am sure you will too." He agreed with his younger brother. "So you're going to try for the archer's medal?"

"Indeed, my good lordling," Asher replied with an older accent and a bow. "Any other contestant will find it quite a challenge to defeat me." He ended with a boast. "And you were invited to sword-dueling and hunting, correct?"

"Fortunately, and unfortunately, yes," Nic replied with a hint of a sigh. Asher smiled and chuckled grimly.

"Then I suppose you will be heading for the archery range next," the younger brother stated.

"I need more than that."

"Indeed, you will. Hunting requires excellent aim, stealth,

the skill of riding a horse, and proficiency at shooting an arrow—something few people have accomplished. I am one of them." Asher smiled smugly. "If you need any hints or aid, just call me."

"Oh, yes, oh, great and wise and old archer!" Nicoron mocked a bow.

"And do not forget the 'old' part," Asher quipped before dodging Nic's quick swipe.

～

Every year when the Helyanwe clan traveled for the Nobling Duels, the family traveled by horseback. On the second day of their three-day journey, they crossed the border. The young dukeling admired the lush forests that sprung up as the clan crossed the Pneutra/Teral border. Tari loved to travel, for she gained an appreciation for the other cantons that made up Levea.

Tari patted the neck of her steed. Prince was a young horse, blacker than midnight with a single white line curling around his ears like a crown. He had earned his name, trotting carefully with a bounce and holding his head high and straight. His ears were perked, and his tail flowed with ease; the dukeling was proud of Prince's regal appearance. The rest of her family had their horses of which they were equally proud, but she felt Prince was the best.

Her bow hung loosely on the horn of her saddle, and her quiver was attached securely on her back. Her sisters also had their bows; Lura wore hers like Tari, but semi-sophisticated Kaete fastened her bow to her waist. According to her, that was a more ladylike place for a quiver. Tari never figured out how a quiver—a weapon basically—could be ladylike in any place. *I suppose that is why we call her semi-sophisticated,* she thought.

Her mind moved to consider the two competitions in which she had to compete—horse-jumping and the horseback-cross-country relay race. The later had been the specialty of the Helyanwe trio for several years. Two teams of three were needed for this particularly thrilling game, and the Helyanwe trio always faced the same opposition—Aster, Astar, and Astair. These triplets of Dakiel, the sons of Master Colodrung, boasted to have the fastest, swiftest horses in Levea, though the sincerity of this remark was unsure. The triplets were also said to be the best riders of their day, and that boast could be verified to an extent. Tari looked forward to competing with the triplets of Dakiel.

Chapter Three

A SOLDIER STRODE confidently through the courtyard of the royal palace of Pneutra with a serious frown on his face. He was young—eighteen or so would have been a safe guess. His white-blonde hair was cut rather short and combed straight back. The patch on his shoulder signified that this young warrior mentored a ten-boy training unit—Training Unit 72, to be precise. To procure the rank of trainer by the age of eighteen was quite an accomplishment, and he had applied himself fully for five years to attain this commission.

He saw every obstacle and objective as a quest with excitement and adventure just beyond the horizon. Most of the other warriors thought of him as boring because he did not laugh at jokes and sing the awful tunes they did (probably because they were a travesty of music). He followed a routine, and nothing would change it, unless, of course, royalty requested something spectacular of him.

"Tanyon? Tanyon Fitherlew?" beckoned a voice from behind him. He turned to see Princess Kanea quickly moving toward him. *Trotting would have been the perfect word for her gait,* he thought as he pushed an unruly lock of his blonde hair out of his eyes. Over the years, he had gained a familiarity with the royal family. Often the princess' guards had to take time off for the Nobling Duels or other such occasions. When that happened, Tanyon and another stepped in.

"Princess," he addressed her with a bow, "what is your request?" A law of Pneutra for any soldier or warrior was to assist the royal family in whatever they might need.

"I need you to tell the sentries that the Langhen countlings and counts should be arriving in the evening. I do not want them to be mistaken for raiders or anyone like that." Tanyon noticed that she seemed out of breath.

"I will do that, your highness," Tanyon replied, the crease on his brow and frown on his mouth still present.

"And I suggest smiling a little. It might make your job easier, not mention preserve your youthfulness." The princess giggled and trotted away. When Tanyon had tried smiling before, he personally thought he looked ridiculous; nevertheless, he tried as the princess had requested. Tanyon turned to the direction of the sentry gate to fulfill his new miniature quest.

The princess plodded into the halls that led to the guest quarters. She began to think about what needed to be done as she sat in one of the decorative and soft chairs in the corridors. *Countlings in tonight, prepare rooms, food…* Kanea's mind trailed off into oblivion as she sat in the chair's embrace.

"Looks like Yoko found his way in your bag again!"

"Yow!" Tari was startled by the familiar sounds emitting from her saddle bag. Lura burst out with laughter.

Even as she spoke, Yoko stuck his head out of the small

opening in Tari's saddlebag. The feline seemed to make it a habit of tailing along for camping trips. He looked at her as if to say, "Hey, this Nobling Duels is a family thing, right?" Tari laughed and softly stroked his head.

"Yoko, you are hopeless if you keep sneaking into my saddlebags when we leave for outings."

Yoko replied in *meowish*, as Tari liked to call it.

Runtron chuckled lightly. "I guess he could enter the scratching competition." That comment made everyone laugh. Prince nickered softly when Yoko climbed expertly out of the saddlebag and perched on the horse's neck, and the cat replied with a purr.

"However," the duke said seriously, "I think we will leave him at Mettrington's Inn when we stop there. It will be better for him there than in the city."

"Not to mention the female cat that lives in the stables," Duchess Reen suggested.

∼

Nicoron blocked a blow from his sparring partner with ease.

"Come now, Denel, are you rusty?" Nicoron taunted. Denel angled his sword to the ground.

"Rusty, no. Tired, yes." He sheathed the sword and continued, "We have been training all morning, Nic."

"You do not want to lose any competitions this year, do you?"

"No, but what is the point of all this training if we are exhausted for the games?" Denel had proved a good point, and Nic finally assented to a rest.

"You could be a lawyer the way you seem to change my mind about everything," Nic noted as he lounged in a chair.

"Changing your mind is not that hard," Denel murmured and tried not to look at the glare he was receiving.

"Let us discuss battle strategies," Nicoron suggested as they rested in the shade of the outdoor pavilion. Servants brought them refreshments, and Nic lifted a goblet to his lips and poured the cool water down his throat. As he put down the cup, Nic saw Asher racing up the stone steps to the pavilion, dodging servants and leaping over shrubbery. Instead of walking normally through the entryway, the boy made a flying launch over the decorative railing and neatly rolled to Nic's feet. The elder lordlings clapped.

"Very well done, Asher the Archer," Denel praised with a smirk. Asher jumped up and dusted off his tunic.

"For once, I like the nickname you chose. Asher the Archer has a nice ring to it," Asher replied. "I like it!"

"Why not Asher the Acrobat?" his elder brother recommended. "Perhaps a better fit with your leap and roll. By the way, what are you doing all the way out here Asher?"

"I was wanting to ask you a question," the boy responded. "Why does every canton have its own name for nobles? I mean, why not just use the same title, since the lords, master, dukes, and counts all have the same rank. So why the different titles?"

The elder opened his mouth to answer, but then shut it. He didn't know why each canton had chosen a different title. *Does it really matter?* Instead of letting his younger brother know of his ignorance, he decided to tease him instead.

"The subject is much too complex for one of your age to understand." He frowned to appear serious, but Asher simply cocked his brow.

"Is that so?" When a smile appeared on his face, Nic knew he was in trouble. "Denel, do you know?"

Denel laughed his thick laugh that reminded Nic of an oak tree's shaking in the wind. "I do not know, and from the looks of it, your big brother doesn't know either. Besides why would you want to know that?" Denel asked, after hearing Nic groan.

"I was planning on a doing a paper for my tutor about the canton social status. Though it seems that Nic's ego is larger than Den's muscles," Asher mocked and raced away to avoid Nic's attempt to snatch him in brotherly play.

Tanyon strode under the inner wall of the citadel's gate and to the outer wall. The double walls allowed for more security than necessary—at least in his opinion. A war had not taken place among the cantons in ages, and having one in the future was not in anyone's mind. Still, the double walls remained. He nodded at the guard at the inner gate and hurried to the stairwell of the outer wall.

When Tanyon reached the top of the stairs, he groaned. Who else but the most annoying warrior in the world—Jakkon Kingerly—would be the sentry at this hour. He groaned, thinking the scrawny man would terrorize anyone given the chance. Gaunt since the day of his birth, his armor made him look even scrawnier. His jet-black hair was reaching an uncomfortable length for Tanyon to even look at, and the elder warrior tried not to think of his clear gray eyes boring into his own pale blue eyes and, oh, that haunting, mischievous grin! Those soul-piercing eyes combined with that grin could sweep fear into the heart of a warrior like the wind sweeps leaves into the house. Breathing a sigh that represented his exasperation, he approached the sentry.

∾

Jakkon's keen eyes scanned the forest for any signs of danger and rubbed his beardless, square chin. He enjoyed the ease of sentry duty. If you see an enemy, you sound the alarm, and then join the archers. Then again, there had not been an enemy for hundreds of years, so standing guard was all he did. In his right hand, he held his favorite weapon of choice—a crossbow, though not a favored weapon in the sight of many, especially in Pneutra. The crossbow made from deer antlers had belonged to his father, who had died when he was about five years of age.

After the death of his father, Jakkon's mother proceeded to work ridiculously long hours in the royal kitchen; as a result, Jakkon suffered from neglect most of his childhood. During the many hours alone, he did one of two things—prank the neighborhood boys who mocked him or read. His escapades, though rather well-planned and executed, had earned him his reputation of an annoying prankster no one wanted to be with. Reading, however, provided him with knowledge not usually granted to warriors and had awakened an unquenchable thirst to become a scribe of Pneutra. Unfortunately, changing occupations in Levea was difficult, nigh onto impossible.

Jakkon caught sight of Tanyon, hesitating at the top of the

outer walls stairwell, and a smirk played its way up his cheek. Tanyon had grown up in the country, Hillsdale to be exact, and did not know of Jakkon's antics until after the move to the citadel. The one difference between the two warriors was that Tanyon's lifestyle had taught him to dislike nonsense, while Jakkon loved pastimes. Since their differences were discovered, the two had tried to keep their distance.

"Tanyon Feather-dew, you cannot hide from me."

Tanyon groaned at this comment. *No wonder few like this individual.*

"It is *Fitherlew*, and you are not a five-year-old boy who cannot pronounce words correctly," Tanyon retorted.

"You are right, I am not of five years, but I cannot resist your reaction. This time was not as exhilarating as when we were younger, but still enjoyable," Jakkon replied mockingly, and Tanyon groaned.

"I am not here to be made a mockery of," Tanyon controlled his anger. "I am here to warn the sentries that the Langhen countlings and counts are to arrive this evening. So don't sound the alarm and shoot the competition." Jakkon laughed.

"Why not? With one canton's noblings out of the way, we have a one out of three chance in winning—a 33-percent chance of winning. If we let them live, we only have a 25-percent chance."

Tanyon rolled his eyes at the statistics. "Of course, but then we'd need to fight Langhen, and peace is more important."

"Of course," Jakkon echoed, and the elder warrior left with a scowl.

If Jakkon would be more of a soldier than a rascal, we might be able to cooperate with ease...but then Jakkon had been like that since a child. Tanyon knew that old habits die hard.

∿

A horn sounded in the night and signaled the arrival of the Langhen countlings and their families. Jakkon looked down to see the well-dressed counts leading the young, strong countlings. The title "count" would have been more appropriate in Jakkon's eyes, for most of the contestants were practically men, not boys. He admired the armor and weapons, and nearly let out a victory cry when he saw a countling proudly holding the reins in one hand and a crossbow in the other. Another sentry strode over to him.

"So I guess you aren't so odd with that whole crossbow fancy and all."

"Indeed, though I would watch your tongue around that countling if I were you." The wielder of a crossbow retorted.

"Why?" the other questioned.

"Did you not recognize him? He was Ghagden Uytil, Count Uytil's eldest son."

"Are not the Uytils the most powerful nobles in Langhen?"

"Correct," Jakkon confirmed, glad that he could impress a fellow soldier, who was obviously perplexed.

"How do you know that it was Ghagden?"

"His armor. Only the Uytils wear the armor made from feather iron." He sniffed. "Only they and the king could afford it."

"Feather iron? How do you know it was feather iron? And what is feather iron."

"*Feather* iron, which is derived from iron, is lighter and stronger than regular iron. One of its major characteristics is that it reflects like a mirror. Ghagden's armor perfectly reflected the lanterns and wall; therefore, it must be feather iron. I hear that the king of Langhen makes full suits of armor of feather iron, then he just stores them."

Perplexed, bewildered and obviously impressed, the sentry left Jakkon standing there.

"Jakkon, one. Opposition, zero." He muttered. A commanding officer approached him, and Jakkon stood to attention.

"Kingerly."

"Sir."

"The princess should be told of the Langhen guests arrival."

"Yes, sir."

"I would like you to take word." The high-ranking officer assigned him to the minuscule task. Jakkon nodded and left the sentry station. After asking a few questions from the maids, he learned where Kanea was last seen and headed for the guest rooms. With the plain layout of the royal palace, finding the guest halls was not difficult. He walked into the hallway and immediately saw the princess asleep in the chair. Jakkon felt uneasy about having to awaken her, but his commander would not be pleased if he ignored the orders. Then again, making physical contact with the royal family without obvious permission was illegal. He was about to tap the princess on the shoulder when he saw something. Jakkon picked up a feather duster that one of the maids had left. *Better than losing my status due to tapping,* he thought.

Feeling something tickling her face, the princess awoke with a start to see feathers in her face. She swept the thing away and then looked up to see who would dare touch her face.

"Princess Kanea," the warrior quickly addressed her. "The Langhen guests have arrived, and please forgive me for the feathering." The princess quickly forgave him.

"I suppose I should greet them." Kanea sighed as she rose from her chair. Jakkon nodded, but after a quick look, he suggested an alternative.

"Perhaps you could have a lady of Pneutra greet them instead, your highness."

"And why would I do that?" Kanea asked as she stood up. "I am the princess and, in absence of king and queen, my duty is to greet the Nobling Duel's contestants. What would the nobles think if we did not perform proper etiquette?"

Jakkon looked to the floor. "I was merely trying to be considerate. You have been working consistently for this upcoming event, and you might be a tad bit exhausted."

Kanea sighed again. "I am exhausted," she admitted, "but my mother would not be pleased if I shirked performing my duty just because I was tired." The solider nodded to show he understood. "Would you please escort me to the guests?" Jakkon bowed and offered the princess his arm.

Chapter Four

THE THIRD DAY of the Helyanwes' trip dawned. On this day all the dukelings of Teral met at Mettrington's Inn. The inn was in Pneutra yet very near Teral and therefore enjoyed the company of the dukes' families every year. Tari especially enjoyed the inn because it was one of the only times she ever saw the other dukelings of Teral. According to her father's calculations, their entourage would arrive in the early afternoon and then have fun with the dukes, duchesses, and dukelings of Teral. Mettrington, the owner and father of the family who ran the inn, would have prepared venison and duck with a savory sauce and the best bread in Levea as they awaited their arrival. She licked her lips at the thought of those delicacies.

The stables of the inn were also very nice, with large stalls and carrots and oats in abundance. What Tari enjoyed most about the stables was the stable girls. The two daughters of Mettrington loved horses and were very kind to them—not to mention they sneaked treats to their guests every time their father's back was turned. The Helyanwe daughters all loved Mettrington's girls, and the two sets had been friends for many years. In their eyes, family status did not matter; Tari liked that only the friendship between them meant something.

"There is the road!" Lura shouted and pointed out the dirt highway that led to Mettrington's Inn and then to the citadel of Pneutra. Tari felt the excitement quicken her, and even Prince's step became lighter and quicker at the sight of it. Yoko yowled in his own excitement. Even he loved the inn, and Tari had a sneaking suspicion that it was because of Mettrington's calico, and that suspicion also went along with the belief that Yoko was the reason that the inn boasted more cats.

～

Nicoron saddled his horse, Thundersbane, in preparation for his family's move to the citadel for the Noblings Duels. Theirs would be half a day's journey to the capital, and the Salindones prided themselves in being early. Nic was excited because they would join with the Quariopels, and he always looked forward to seeing Denel.

"Nic, a little help?" Asher asked after a little trouble saddling his own horse. Nic smiled and replied.

"I am almost done with Thundersbane." He tightened the cinch underneath the silver horse. When he had finished, he patted Thundersbane's neck and went to aid his little brother. Asher had a shorter-sized horse which made up for his size in attitude.

"Thanks, Nic, I do not know why, but Lightning does not seem to want to stay still so I can saddle him." His elder brother laughed.

"Lightning never wants to stay still, Asher. He's a very spirited animal."

"Which is why I wanted him and not the other slow pony."

Asher smiled and scratched his horse under the chin. Nicoron handed him the bridle.

"Get this on your horse, or else you will never control him." A mischievous grin appeared on the brother's face.

"Of course," Ash replied, but he continued to scratch Lightning's chin. As Asher began to vigorously scratch the horse's chin, Nic observed the horse extend his neck straight, obviously relishing the attention. Soon the horse's mouth was open and the tongue lolling out; then Asher strapped on the bridle.

"Interesting technique," Nic commented.

"Indeed, but it is the only way I can get the bit in his mouth." Lightning snorted in protest, but the bit stayed in his mouth.

"He doesn't seem very happy, though," Nic observed.

"I know," Asher replied with a sad tone, "I wish I could get a bridle without a bit for him." The boy patted Lightning's neck and stroked his forehead. Nic was confused.

"Is there even such a bridle made?"

"I heard of one in Dakiel. An inventor found a horse that had been beaten and mistreated, and he took the horse in to nurse it back to health. When the horse was strong enough, the boy tried to ride it, but the horse would not take to a bridle." Nicoron knew what was next.

"So this inventor invented a bridle without a bit."

"Exactly. I thought it was an amazing idea."

"Indeed, those Dakiel people are talented with their horses," he replied in admiration. "My hat's off to him." The lordling turned to give Thundersbane more attention when he heard a familiar voice.

"Who is your hat off to?" Lord Nanook asked.

"Hello, Father," Asher greeted. "We were discussing that inventor from Dakiel."

"The one who invented the strange bridle?" their father asked, and Nic assured him that he was correct. Nanook patted the neck of Nicoron's horse.

"I see why one would admire him." The lord then changed the subject. "And how are my sons' steeds?" Thundersbane nickered boldly to answer a positive answer. "Looks like Thunder is doing great." He chuckled. "Now what about Lightning?" Asher's smaller horse snorted and stamped in protest to his bridle. When his father inquired about the horse's negative attitude, Asher explained and added how much he would like to procure the special bridle for his horse. Lord Nanook smiled.

"I see" was all he said for the moment. Nic began to fasten Thundersbane's bridle on him. A few moments of silence passed except for the slapping of leather and clanking of metal. The lord then turned to his sons.

"Where is my horse?"

Barely suppressing a chuckle, Nicoron replied, "Jackrabbit is in the meadow." Asher didn't try to suppress his own laughter at the name of his father's horse.

"*Jackrabbit*? Father, wherever did you come up with that name?"

"Jackrabbits did exist, son." Lord Nanook explained. "They were creatures about six feet tall and were mostly like giant rabbits. Their claws dug huge tunnels in the grounds. Also, they lived in groups called *bandas*, and the leader would have antlers. It was said that the antlers of the lead jackrabbit were more beautiful that any deer in Pneutra." He paused to take a breath. "Jackrabbits were the fastest creatures ever to set paw on Levea's soil, and I named my steed after them for that very reason." Nicoron nodded. He could understand choosing a horse's name associated with speed, but he preferred something a bit more heroic—Thundersbane fit it perfectly.

What would girls think if I rode a horse named "Jackrabbit"? he thought. *They'd probably do that laughing sort of thing to its name. I'm positive they wouldn't laugh at a horse by the strong name of Thundersbane.* The cocky youth was aroused from his thoughts when a servant announced that the Lady Nan was prepared for the journey, and that message motivated him to finish preparing his horse. His father and younger brother continued to talk about jackrabbits.

"So you named your horse after something whose existence is questionable?" he heard Asher ask.

"Just because I have never seen a jackrabbit and your grandfather never saw one doesn't mean they didn't exist." Nanook defended his beliefs, though he could tell that neither of his sons would ever believe him. They exchanged a few more words, and then Nanook surrendered his case. *Seriously,* Nicoron thought, *a giant rabbit with antlers? Now that possibility is a laugh.*

～

Kanea awoke that morning with one thought: Pneutraite lordlings and Dakielite masterlings were arriving that day! She fell back on her soft luxurious pillow and groaned. Perhaps her mother would appear that day and aid her—even just a little. A knock on her door caused her to sit up.

"Kanea darling," her mother's voice called through the door. The princess smiled at the welcoming sound and disregarding that she was still in her nightgown, she quickly rose and skipped to the door to open it. Queen Aan walked in and embraced her only daughter.

"I have heard about how hard you have worked and prepared for the foreign noblings arrival. I'm proud of your stepping up to responsibility when I could not." Another hug was in order. "Now I want you to take the day off and do something fun. I think you really need the break."

"Thank you, Mother!" Kanea squealed. The queen smiled and left the room, reminding Kanea to be in by supper and not to get too sunburned. Kanea ran to her closet and took out a green archery suit. The elongated jerkin had gold threads weaved into the fabric, making a lovely ivy pattern. Then she donned on some alleged dragon-hide boots. Her father had bought them for her when she first became interested in archery though he admitted that for them to be made of dragon hide or to be as old as the seller portrayed them to be would be impossible. "Dragons left Levea hundreds of years ago, and would you look at these boots. They look like they came straight from the cobbler's shop! No, I do not believe for a second that they are constructed of dragon hide." And Kanea believed her father. As she gazed at the boots, she found herself thinking of her father. Tears welled up in her eyes.

She looked in the mirror. Today she might have considered herself just a tad stunning; she never looked at herself as even remotely beautiful, but every other person in the kingdom thought so. Kanea could understand her mother's saying so, but mothers were often biased. Subjects said so because it was common knowledge that the queen and princesses were the models of the kingdom, so beauty was based upon them. Kanea frowned; she had never liked that part of being royalty.

～

"Right on schedule, Duke Runtron." Mettrington walked out in his dingy, yet clean, apron and greeted the Helyanwes. "Chorta, Filica," he called his two daughters, "we have guests!" Tari slid off Prince, and Yoko leaped on her shoulder and then onto the ground when he saw Mettrington's calico right behind Chorta and Filica. The cats ran off into the barn as the two sets of girls walked the horses into the barn.

Cheery conversation arose during the grooming of the horses, and the stable girls wished the Helyanwe trio luck in their games. They parted, and the trio rejoined their parents. The evening continued with reunions with the other nobles of Teral, luscious meals in Mettrington's dining hall, and other enjoyable pastimes. Tari enjoyed hearing stories from the other nobles about past Nobling Duels and even some tales about dangerous sea voyages. One duke told the infamous tale of his voyage around the entire circumference of Levea. The journey, which required two years, was well worth the time and effort. What most interested the young nobles was the duke's in-depth description of Crakaton's coasts as he passed the mysterious land.

"The rugged mountains that met us clearly warned us of

the treacherous land. We were careful about the sea stacks protruding out of the gray sea. The unusually strong currents seemed to possess an ill will and wished to pull us into the rugged rocks. Over the mountains, I could see what might have been King Trea San's former fortress." He paused for a breath and then continued, "And can I forget the fabled volcanoes that I saw over the crags above the sea?" Tari tried to picture the stony projections, the gray sea, and billowing smoke rising above it all.

"During our voyage," the duke continued, "I had the privilege of standing on the lookout as we passed the coast, and I beheld a mysterious sight. Set in the clefts of the mountains facing us was a small, wooden structure. *Strange*, I thought, *that a structure of any sort should be in such a precarious position.* Stranger yet was the smoke snaking out of a chimney." Tari was baffled; a hut built in the clefts of treacherous mountains with smoke coming out of it? She looked around the room and realized she was not the only one. One person spoke up.

"Do you think someone could have been foolhardy enough to live on the edge of mountains—especially those?" a voice countered. The night continued with stories, but soon the young dukeling began to become tired and had to retire to her quarters. All three girls slept in the same huge bed, which normally would have heard the chatter of their discussing the day, but tonight they were too tired. Yoko left his calico friend and joined the trio in their bed, taking his usual spot between the girls' feet.

Chapter Five

TEN BOYS SIMULTANEOUSLY raised their bows, drew back on the bowstring, and let go at the command of their captain. Tanyon was proud of his boys' progress. Their ages ranged from ten to twelve and were the perfect age for Tanyon's patience level, which was rather slim at times. This was his first battalion to train in all the arts of war, but previously he had the honor of teaching Princess Kanea.

Their archery skills can use some work, he thought with an inward groan as he saw arrows fall short of the target, fly past the target, or barely hit the target. Kanea was a natural when it came to aim.

"Good effort," he told them honestly, knowing that his students only did their best. "Keep practicing on that aim. Now, draw." Each student drew an arrow from the supply provided. "Prepare." With his bow pointed toward the ground, each boy nocked his arrow to the bowstring and rested the shaft on the arrow rest. "Aim." The boys lifted their bows, pinpointing their target. "Fire!"

~

Kanea saw brown streaks fly through the air and heard the thud of some hitting the targets as well as the scraping sound of arrows striking the stone ground. She chuckled a little when she saw some of the boys grimacing at their results.

"Good effort," she heard Tanyon say with a little stress. She stepped up to the royal archery platform, above all the other archery lines. The platform was constructed out of wood, and the target was sturdy with unique colors, unlike the normal targets. Kanea waved at her attendant. As she took aim, Kanea felt as if someone were staring at her. She looked down and realized that Tanyon's students were waiting for her to shoot. Shrugging, she aimed her arrow, released it, and it hit very close to the middle. The boys clapped in admiration. Kanea turned to them and bowed elegantly.

Tanyon smiled as he saw his former student do well. The student closest to him asked. "The princess was your student, correct?"

"Indeed, she was," he answered.

"Think we will ever be as good as her?"

"If you work as hard as she did, you might," he assured the young boy.

Impressed by their willingness to practice, Kanea subtly observed her former teacher working with Training Unit 72. As she watched from her royal range, she saw another person on the far part of the court. Squinting, Kanea realized it was Jakkon, the sentry who had alerted her about the arrival of the Langhen guests. He did not seem to want to be noticed and stayed to himself, practicing with his crossbow. Kanea had seen one of the foreign noblings wield one, but never a person in Pneutra. Much intrigued by his choice, she resolved to ask him about it.

The archery lessons continued until the yellow light of afternoon began to give way to the paler hue of evening. Tanyon had been instructed to let his students return to the dormitories before nightfall, and he did not wish to cross his own commander. He knew that it would take time to store away the weapons before allowing the student to return; therefore, now would be the best time to discontinue his lessons.

"Lessons are finished for today, students," he announced as evening began to settle in. Cheers of joy were their reply. Kanea watched Tanyon take the young ones to the armory, probably wanting to be sure the weapons were properly cared for. She eyed Jakkon at the far end of the court.

Tanyon had not paid much attention to the man, much to his own relief. Once Tanyon and Training Unit 72 left the field, she padded down the wooden stairs and began to walk toward the far end. She greeted him, perhaps a bit shyly.

"Good evening, Princess Kanea Ilindel," he responded as he loaded his crossbow again and fired.

"I was wondering about your weapon," she said, and Jakkon nodded. She cleared her throat. "What is it?" she asked.

The sentry turned and looked her in the eyes, and she was taken aback at his breach of protocol. Most of her subjects would merely look to the ground—not straight into her eyes. Instead of being upset though, she felt for the first time she wasn't being viewed as "Princess Kanea" but as merely Kanea.

"It is a handheld crossbow invented by a man in Teral. The

weapon was originally made for spearfishing, but then a modified version was put on citadel walls. Finally, the inventors came up with a handheld variation."

"Are there any specific advantages the handheld crossbow has over the regular bow?"

"Yes, actually there are a few advantages. One would be that it holds the bolt for you, then you not are expending energy holding the string. It is heavy, therefore, it can also be used as a mace if you happen to run out of bolts during a battle. It also gives more force to the bolt than an archer could give to an arrow." He handed it to Kanea for her to see how heavy it was, and she wholly agreed with Jakkon.

"You call your arrows *bolts*. Why?"

"Bolts are made differently than arrows." He pulled a bolt from his quiver and instructed her to do the same. Jakkon held each side by side, and Kanea could see that the bolt was shorter than the arrow and lacked feathers on its end. The warrior looked to the sky.

"I should be returning to my quarters," he abruptly stated.

Kanea agreed. "Thank you very much for the clarifications."

"My pleasure." Then he was gone. Kanea skipped back to the royal range and picked up her belongings. As she turned to leave, she saw Tanyon.

"Good evening, Tanyon," she greeted.

"Good evening, Princess. Your archery has improved even since we had your last lesson."

"I have the urge to practice," she replied. "Your boys are coming along wonderfully."

"Thank you, though I do think they would have to work twice as hard as you did, my lady. You were a prodigy in the sport."

Kanea giggled at his compliment. "I think that was partly because I had nothing but practicing to do all day. Your boys do not have that kind of time."

"Indeed, but I still think you had an unknown talent." Tanyon smiled down at her. She was quite beautiful for her age, and he found it difficult not to stare. "Well, should we call it a night?"

"What a perfect idea," Kanea replied as she slung her bow over her shoulder. The warrior chuckled as he remembered her learning that trick from him. "Would you kindly escort me to the palace, Tanyon?" He bowed and offered her his arm.

"Indeed."

Thundersbane bucked violently when Nicoron pulled his bit too hard.

"Sorry, boy, but you are too pigheaded." Asher laughed hard as the horse bucked yet again.

"I think you might need one of those bit-less bridles," he commented, and though Denel found it hard to suppress a chuckle, he did out of loyalty. Nic loosened his grip, and Thundersbane gave a thankful nicker and moved along happily.

He looked up into the evening sky to see some of the most beautiful colors ever produced by nature. Lavender-lined clouds were sparse against the orange sky that faded into blues still higher. The yellow faded against the horizon into the orange which faded into the blue. He knew within minutes the sky would be black, and guessing by the cloud cover, the stars would be very bright tonight. One of Nic's favorite kind of nights was a cloudless night that allowed the stars to be very pronounced.

"Beautiful night, is it not?" a fatherly sounding voice interrupted Nicoron's reverie.

"Indeed, Father," he responded.

"I can name five of the constellations," Asher boasted and began to name the certain ones in his knowledge. "And the last one is Shadrious, the sailor, and those four stars represent his ship. He is in the north."

"Very well done, Asher," his father praised. Denel decided to show off some of his own knowledge.

"But I feel sure you did not know that the faint star at the top of Shadrious' shoulder is his parrot."

Nicoron just laughed at the smug smile on Denel's face. "I am really surprised at the imagination of the ancient stargazers. I mean I could have never paired all of those different star patterns with all of those actual happenings."

Denel chuckled at the retort.

"I guess they just had nothing better to do back then," Asher mused.

"Indeed." Nic breathed. The rest of their journey to the capital citadel was uneventful. Occasional conversations began then died soon after, for the travelers were too tired to continue. Personally, Nicoron felt excited to return to his duty as guard and was even more excited when his mind settled on the Nobling Duels. Thoughts of running the other competing noblings out of the arena with the help of his best friend basically entertained his weary mind.

⁓

Kanea admired her tan at the end of the day. Her arms were the perfect shade of brown, and it covered the blemishes on her face, compliments of adolescence. Her hair had lightened quite nicely, and she felt like she was all ready to present herself to the noblings. Tonight, the lordlings were scheduled to arrive at Pneutra's citadel, marking the end of the droves of nobles who would be traveling along the highways for the beginning of the Nobling Duels. *Watching the games again will be exciting,* Kanea thought. *I wonder who will be winners this year. Almost every nobling had something to take home, but the wonder of who would lead the winners was on many minds.*

The princess would have bet on Ghagden, that is, if her mother's speeches on all of the reasons why princesses should not place bets did not ring in her ears. She had seen the countling practicing in the archery range every day all day, and he was excellent in the ways of the crossbow. Kanea had even heard Jakkon compliment him often. The princess breathed a sigh of relief that she did not have to greet the noblings tonight, and that her mother was taking care of the rest. In the morning, she would join her mother in hosting all of the noblings for beginning of the Nobling Duels. Kanea closed her eyes and fell into oblivion.

⁓

Tari had arrived in Pneutra's capital that day and was enjoying seeing the sights again. She and her sisters loved simply walking around the city, through the market, and underneath the highway bridges. Lura's favorite place was the market and the vendors there that sold all sorts of interesting things. Kaete absolutely adored the town square with its gorgeous shrubs and lanterns that glowed in the evening like giant fireflies. Tari's favorite place by far was the archery range. In Teral, archery was not a dominant sport, so the ranges were not as exquisite as the range she enjoyed in Pneutra.

The walk was relaxing after their trip, and Tari enjoyed the extra time with her elder sisters. As night wore on, the noblings enjoyed reuniting with the foreign nobles for soon the peace that existed would soon be removed by the games.

"Tari, Lura, look!" Kaete pointed to a rather handsome and bulky nobling. "That is Ghagden Uytil, the crossbow wielder."

"So?" Lura asked, being more interested in the fruits that were indigenous to Pneutra.

"Ghagden Uytil is the best archer of our age group. He has won the golden award for archery every year since he was five years old!" Tari could see Kaete was an avid fan.

Teasingly the youngest said, "You do know that unions between people of different cantons are very rare and rather discouraged, right, Kaete?"

The elder glared at the younger. "You're taking this the wrong way," she objected. "It is merely that he is a very good archer and deserves to be recognized."

"I think he would get enough recognition from his own nobles," Lura noted as she returned from the fruit vendor. "By the way, who are we talking about?"

Kaete sighed. "Lura, you're amazing" was all the eldest said. Tari clarified that she had only been jesting.

"I know what you mean," she paused as she smiled mischievously, "I think."

Kaete looked as if she were about pounce on Tari, like Yoko did with his toy mouse. "Do not worry about it. I just thought that it was interesting that I would be competing with him this year," Kaete continued.

The middle of the group spoke up as she took a bite from her fruit. "If he's been an archer since he was five, then have not we competed with him before?"

"Yes, I suppose, but it is just now I am realizing who he is," Kaete replied.

"You mean an enemy," Lura responded.

"What do you mean *an enemy*? He isn't trying to overthrow Langhen's government or cheat people out of their earnings!" the other exploded.

"Mayhap, but the very fact that he is from Langhen makes him an enemy."

Kaete was dumbfounded by Lura's statements until her sister clarified her comments. "Do you not really see what I mean, Kaete? Ghagden is a competitor, which makes him a bad guy to us."

The eldest was not impressed with her sister's logic. "Just because someone is competing against you doesn't make him your enemy," she argued tersely.

"Maybe not for you, but it does for me," Lura replied as she took another bite out of her fruit.

Tari sighed. The elder two often had discussions like this, and she was usually the one to calm down everyone.

"Lura, Kaete, let's not have this conversation again. Ghagden is a fellow nobling; therefore, we should display courtesy to him. Yet we should not allow our emotions to stand in front of our determination to win the games." Tari looked at Kaete with suspicion and was rewarded with a roll of her sister's eyes.

Chapter Six

MORNING WAS BUSTLING and loud. Noblings were fitting themselves in the armory, and their guardians were giving them speeches. Tanyon had heard many of them in the past years, and he, being the host of the armory, was hearing many of them over again. Jakkon was also there. Tanyon groaned, but instead of dwelling on the other's presence, he continued to aid a young nobling who had acquired a serious case of nervousness. He tried to encourage the young one but encouraging another wasn't one of his strong traits.

Nicoron and Denel had one last spar before the games. Asher clapped at the performance.

"I think you two are ready," he teased.

"We had better be," Denel assented, "because the sword-fighting duels begin soon."

"Then we should go and prepare our armor and weapons," Nic suggested.

Asher ran into the bleachers to accompany his parents. A few minutes later, the announcer signaled for the contestants to walk into the arena. This was the most exciting moment for Nicoron. The thrill of seeing the people who were going to witness their superior skills was overwhelming to him. He was sure every nobling who strode out into the center of the arena felt the same way.

∽

The Helyanwe trio were among the spectators; they would have never missed a fight.

"Greetings!"

Tari whirled to see who called them and made a noise that sounded like part groan, part laugh. *Who could it be other than the Dakiel triplets?* Their names were about as similar as their faces, stature, and clothing. The eldest (by five minutes) was taller by a quarter of an inch, and he made the most of it. The other two flanked his sides with mischievous smiles playing across their faces.

"Astair, Astar, and Aster…looking forward to being whipped again?" Lura taunted.

"Not this year, Lura, so don't get your hopes up," Astair, the eldest, replied with a laugh.

"So I assume you have a plan," Tari jumped in. There was no ill will between the trios—only a competitive spirit.

"Actually, we do," Astar and Aster responded in unison.

"And it is a good one…" their leader added as he looked down on all three girls.

"Good!" Kaete smiled. "Because we got a better one."

Tari suppressed a giggle at her sister's confident comment. *She has such a way with words.*

∽

Kanea was ecstatic. Queen Aan had just announced that

Kanea would be the one to shoot the starting arrow, and the time had come. Crowds were packed into the arena, and if it were not for the royal box that had been designated for royalty, the princess was quite sure that there would not be any room for them.

"Kanea Ilindel, would you do the honors?" Aan smiled as she motioned for the princess to signal the beginning of the games. She reached for her bow and an arrow. Aiming carefully, she looked for the mark on the far wall where the arrow was supposed to hit. Then she let go. The arrow smoothly flew and hit its designated mark.

"Let the games begin!" boomed the announcer.

Chapter Seven

ANYON WAS IMPRESSED with the skill displayed by the contestants in the first duel. He was not sure of the contenders' names, but he could decipher their nativity by the bright-colored capes that adorned their shoulders. Langhenian countlings flaunted crimson capes; Teralian dukelings dressed in a teal color; Dakielite masterlings wore a golden cape, and Pneutraite lordlings displayed the symbol of their nation, the forest green. The nobling from Teral easily evaded the other's strikes but was slow to give his own. *A rookie,* Tanyon thought. An experienced competitor would not be so hesitant. The competition ended in the triumph of the Dakiel. The warrior heard a noise and looked up to see Jakkon.

"Greetings," the crossbow wielder said as he took the only seat left—one next to Tanyon.

"Greetings," the elder mumbled. He wished he could be somewhere else—anywhere else.

"Forgive me for interrupting your peaceful sitting, but I could not find another seat within the whole auditorium," Jakkon said.

Tanyon nodded. "Forget it. I could be sitting next to the opposition."

"True, at least we're on the same team."

"Indeed." Tanyon left it to that. He really did not want to converse.

⁓

Nicoron waited with great anticipation for their performance in the makeshift armory adjacent to the open arena. The armory was a great place to catch up with friends from foreign cantons and to observe the strategies of the other challengers, Asher's personally given duty.

Nic laughed as he saw his younger brother mask his face with charm and approach the other participants. Truly, the younger Salidone was quite charming and made friends easily; besides, Nic appreciated the facts that his little brother gathered. He had found the information very useful in the past, and he had no doubt of its usefulness this year. Denel felt guilty about using Asher's scouting.

"It is cheating, Nic," he would protest.

"It is not cheating…" Nic would counter, "only strategy of our own. Real war works just like this."

Denel still felt guilty. His thoughts were then interrupted by his brother's tackle.

"What!" Nic yelled as he went down. "What is that for?"

"Your turn for the dueling is come!" Asher shouted in his face. The nobling hurried to the exit. Denel was there waiting.

"Do you know who our competition is?" Nic asked. His friend nodded.

"Langhenian fighters," he replied.

"You make them sound like fierce warriors."

"Langhenians aren't exactly known for fear."

"Truer words were never spoken." Nic smiled. Then the horn, signaling their entrance, was blown. The noblings smiled faded when he spotted the Langhen competition. They were muscular, and their armor was amazing.

"Feather iron," Denel whispered to him.

Not encouraging, Denel, Nic thought but chose not to share his thoughts. He feared those words would reduce their morale.

"Means nothing," was all he mumbled as they approached the "enemy." As per tradition, they met in the middle of the arena and respectfully bowed to each other. A referee met them and spewed the rules as he did at every game and then left. Each contestant pulled out his sword and performed the usual courtesy, merely holding his sword upright in front of his face. If Nic cared to ask anyone about the reason for the action, the person would have answered that the gesture was to signify no ill will. Then the game began.

Kanea watched with enthusiasm. It thrilled her that her own guards were battling the fearless Langhenians! She was probably making more out of it than necessary, but she thought Nic was a nice person. He had protected her, though there had been no reason for the protection—at least there hadn't been until the past few weeks when that strange creature had attacked and mercilessly executed her father. She tried not to think of the tragedy that had recently come to her land. Instead she focused on the duel that was before her.

One thing about being royalty was that they got the best

seat in the whole arena, best views and everything. Nicoron's friend seemed to be doing just fine, but Nic seemingly was out-matched and in trouble.

~

Mental note: never ignore your best friend's sayings, Nic thought as he tried to keep blocking his opponent's smooth attacks. *This warrior is too good! No way any noblings could be this good!* His opposition was fast and powerful. He attacked unrelenting, even though he may not have made the best of moves, Nic was overwhelmed simply trying to block them. He racked his brain for any secret strategies or maybe some of Asher's information. One feint came to mind, and he groaned at the idea of using his father's secret. The ploy required retreating before making the winning move. Retreating was not his kind of sport but retreating for a while was better than losing completely. He made exactly five even steps backward.

~

Kanea was confused. She knew Nicoron good enough to know he would not retreat. *What is he doing?* she wondered.

~

Tanyon grunted in disgust when he saw the quick retreat. He knew Nicoron from training, and he seemed like a good fighter. Watching his retreat was painful.

"Tell me, Jakkon, is this coward one of our boys?"

"Yes," Jakkon replied, very much surprised that he would even ask him a question willingly. "You must be in dire straits to be asking me," he said.

"I am. This is trying my heart and soul," Tanyon moaned.

∽

Nicoron timed his feint perfectly. The five steps backward caused the opponent to lunge at him. Nic made two quick steps to the right, and the countling fell.

∽

Jakkon howled in laughter and surprise. Tanyon removed his hands from his eyes.

"What happened? Is Lordling Nicoron down yet?" Tanyon snapped to attention to ensure the fate of the poor lordling.

"You should have seen that slick move!" Jakkon tried to explain what Nic had executed but then turned to just howl again, this time with the rest of the crowd.

∽

Kanea sat looking on in awe and admiration. Nicoron's adroit moves made the Langhen warrior look like a fumbling fool. The first side moves were too fast for anyone to truly understand what was going on. His clever feint happened all too quickly, but his second move demanded cheers from everyone.

∽

Tari laughed when she saw the Pneutraite nobling at first struggle and then retreat.

"Look at that coward!" she said all too soon. Nic's technique and footage knocked the wind out of their lungs.

"Kaete, if you are looking for some foreign nobling to marry, try that one first!" Lura blurted.

"Indeed" was all Kaete could muster.

∽

Nicoron breathed a little heavier. At least he had the

crowd's approval, but the Langhenian was not ready to give up what had started out to be his game. He reared from the dusty stone and swung his sword around in both hands before giving Nicoron a look that could make him mincemeat. Nicoron stood ready. As the other charged in rage, Nic made several swift moves. For his last move, he made one strong down blow, knocking the sword completely out of his opponent's hand. He breathed heavily. The technique worked, but it required skill and strength, mostly at the end. Nicoron looked up to see the crowd cheering; obviously, he had won. He glanced at Denel and the Langhenian's partner. Both were just gawking at him.

⁓

Kanea clapped and cheered wildly for the Pneutraite team.

"Nicoron has done well, has he not?" Queen Aan commented to her daughter.

"Very much so," Kanea replied breathlessly.

⁓

Tanyon was so much in awe that he began laughing.

"You didn't expect that did you, Feather-dew?" Jakkon mumbled to him, but the cheering was so loud that Tanyon did not hear the annoying nickname that the younger sentry had labeled him.

"No, I did not expect it." Tanyon breathed.

⁓

The Helyanwe trio was going crazy. Each of them was talking at the same time, and so none of them knew what the other was trying to say. Tari quit speaking and watched as the Pneutraite duo received an award for their excellent swordsmanship. Her eyes wondered to the royal booth where the princess and queen sat with their guards and a young dark-headed girl whom Tari assumed to be an assistant.

~

As Nic and Denel retreated to the armory, they were met by cheers and fans from the stands.

"Looks like everybody loved your secret move." Denel laughed as he punched Nic in the arm. Within the five-minute break, the armory was swarmed with people, and Nic was glad when they finally left to see the next duel. Denel notified his best friend that he was going to clean up and change. "After that workout, I am exhausted."

Nic just nodded as he cleaned his sword. "Do you think I impressed any girls?" Nicoron asked his friend.

Denel stuck out his head from around the corner. "Why would you ask that?" His right eyebrow was raised in his usual suspicious manner.

"Curious," Nic replied blandly.

Curious, eh? Well, I am curious about why you're curious, Denel thought. *In many ways, Nic is almost hopeless.*

"Maybe, maybe not." Then he escaped from the room before he could be asked any more awkward questions. Nic, on the other hand, was deep in his thoughts, yet not really thinking about his question.

"Hello, Nicoron Salindone," came a lovely voice from behind him. He turned to see a black-headed girl about his age, looking up at him.

"Uh, hi," he stuttered. Thin, pink lips smiled at him and

mesmerizing violet eyes fluttered. "Do you want to see the next duel?" Nic asked cautiously.

"And why would I do that when I would like to see the nobling who just performed impeccable sword-fighting in person?"

Nic blushed slightly and was very flattered. *I guess performing impeccable sword-fighting does produce attention.*

"Uh, thank you. Uh, what is your name?" he asked the smiling girl. Now that he was finally confronted with a girl like he wanted, Nic was speechless.

"Dibla."

"Any clan name?"

"No." She looked down, and her voice quivered. "I was orphaned and abandoned, so I have no idea what my surname is." Dibla looked up into his eyes with her teary own. Nicoron's heart went out to her. Footsteps sounded through the halls.

"I have need to leave," Dibla stated, and before Nic could blink, she was gone. He leaned against the wall and sighed.

Chapter Eight

THE SECOND DAY of the Nobling Duels was what some people referred to as "Horsey Day." Competitions requiring horses were performed. This day, which was Tari's favorite, was also the day that the Helyanwe trio and Dakiel triplets rose to combat in the cross-country final. At least, that was the assumption of many. For years, the two sets of three had risen to the finals and raced each other in relay-race style the next day. Both sets had won intermittently. The dukelings looked forward to the competitions.

In the warriors' cabins, the talk dwelt on the previous day's games. Nicoron had easily become a hero to many of the trainees-of-war. Before morning had expired, Tanyon heard, "He's amazing!" enough times to last for ten days of rejoicing. Jakkon lounged in his upper cot, listening to the others' discussing the hero of the swordsmanship competition but remained silent. Tanyon was among them and joined in the conversation.

"Lordling Nicoron was very impressive yesterday," stated one warrior.

"Not you too!" cried another. "I have heard every single trainee-of-war mention how awesome and amazing he is."

"Me too," Tanyon agreed. "I cannot get any of Training Unit 72 to be quiet about it."

"I guess children need a hero occasionally," stated another.

Jakkon grunted. He wished he had had a chance to have a hero in his life.

"What was that stunt he did?" inquired a new warrior.

"I do not know," Tanyon replied.

"A mystery move, I bet," added the newcomer.

"You are close," Jakkon said quietly. Tanyon looked up.

"You think you know something about this?" he asked, and Jakkon huffed.

"It is well-known that every clan has their own secret stunt. Clearly, Lordling Nicoron put his own into use at the right moment." He gazed around the room. *Silence. Good,* he thought, *some information is in order.* He continued, "Nobles have been leaders in war for as long as anyone can remember; therefore, they must have some sort of clan strategy passed from generation to generation. Some moves are similar, but each one is different in its own way." He paused for a breath and was interrupted by Tanyon.

"How do you know this?" the elder asked.

"I read in my spare time. The library contains many old books and records," he added quietly, "and I listen to the gossip in the town square."

The listeners considered his words. The moment of silence that prevailed would have continued had the newcomer not burst into laughter. The others stared at him. He eventually stopped, and an awkward silence returned to the room.

A bell from the courtyard signaled the beginning of the events. Jakkon was thankful for the save. *Saved by the bell,* he thought as he followed the rest of the warriors outside. Some said they were going to work out, and others proclaimed they were going to witness the games. Others said they had plans. Jakkon was deciding what to do when a maid approached him, a rare occurrence for him.

"Jakkon Kingerly and Tanyon Fitherlew?" asked the maid timidly. Jakkon was unaware that Tanyon was behind him and was startled when he heard his voice from behind saying, "Yes, that is us."

"The queen requests that you two escort the princess to and from today's games. As you can understand she would be nervous about letting her daughter beyond the citadel walls without proper security, even though the *incident* was far from here."

"We can understand," Tanyon replied.

Does this man not think I can talk for myself? Jakkon had to wonder.

"Of course, we can do that," Jakkon added. Once he had spoken, he wondered why he had agreed to protect the Princess Kanea Ilindel with Tanyon. *What am I thinking?* he wondered but then reminded himself that he was being offered a supreme duty only given to a few. *I guess I will have to deal with it.*

～

Tari was busy fashioning some braids in Prince's mane.

"You are actually braiding your stallion's mane?" Lura asked incredulously.

"Yes, to keep the mane from flying in my face when we are galloping."

"But Prince is a male horse!"

"He is a horse! He does not care whether or not his mane is braided!" Tari retorted.

"But he is a male!" Lura objected. Kaete stepped in.

"Girls, let us not have discord before the game. We need all the teamwork we can muster if we're going to win." The elder settled the matter.

"I still cannot believe you're putting braids in a boy's hair," Lura murmured.

"No discord," Tari replied smugly.

Kanea waited anxiously for her favorite day—"Horsey Day" to begin. She loved seeing the beautiful horses race around the arena and perform various stunts. These competitions were held in a smaller arena deep in the woods, where the sports requiring hunting would be easier. What she loved even more was the very last competition—the cross-country race. The two undefeated teams through the day's games were chosen to compete against each other. She knew as well as many others that the Dakiel triplets and a Teralian sister team were favored to compete in the only cross-country competition. As to who would win that, she did not know, nor did she care to guess.

A maid entered her room to announce that her guards had been appointed.

"The queen wanted you to have two warriors to guard you, since your proper guard will be competing."

"Very well," Kanea assented, "who are the warriors?"

"Jakkon Kingerly and Tanyon Fitherlew."

"Wonderful!" Kanea replied and clasped her hands. "I know both of those warriors."

"I will go prepare your horse for your journey" offered the maid.

"Oh, thank you! I nearly forgot about that." She smiled at the servant and was pleased with her return smile. The princess turned to go but stopped, thought for one moment, and then went to collect her bow and quiver.

"Maid, please take this bow and quiver to be used in starting the games," she ordered.

∽

Nicoron prepared his horse for the journey to the forest arena. Thundersbane impatiently stamped his foot.

"Do not worry, boy. I am eager for a good hunting chase as well," he assured the steed with a pat on the neck. "We will get ourselves a nice fat buck with huge antlers, and I will have even more girls around me than ever before." If Nic believed that animals could understand every word that one spoke, he would have insisted that his horse nickered in agreement.

"As if you ever had any girls around you in the first place."

Alas, it was not his horse, but his little brother who displayed this attitude of disparagement.

"Asher."

"Brother!" Asher replied as he found Lightning's stall.

"Do you have Lightning ready?'

"Indeed! Lightning is the best jumper this world has ever

seen, and we're going to display that ability in full view of every spectator in Levea today." Lightning reared in his stall as if to augment Asher's statement. Nicoron smiled.

"I hope you beat them all," he said with a brotherly hair ruffling.

Asher chuckled as he swatted away Nic's annoying hand. "Me too," he added.

A horn sounded signaling that people were preparing to leave for the smaller stadium.

~

Tanyon took the role of understood leader and immediately began to bark orders to Jakkon.

"Go and secure our horses," he instructed. "I will go escort the princess to the stables and meet you at the entrance where you will have our horses saddled and ready to go." Before Jakkon could object, Tanyon hurried off to the royal chambers.

Jakkon shrugged and followed the instructions—not because Tanyon told him to, but because he was fulfilling his special duty to the beautiful Princess Kanea.

Tanyon did not get far when he met the princess outside the royal house. "Princess Kanea, I have instructions from—"

Kanea cut him short. "Oh, I know Tanyon. You and Jakkon are supposed to escort me to the woodland arena and back. Now let us be off with it now, or else we'll miss the troop." She skirted past him and trotted off to the stables. *She's trotting again!* he thought as he worked to keep up with her without looking ludicrous.

"Shouldn't you and Jakkon have weapons?" Kanea suddenly asked. Tanyon stopped dead. *I hadn't even thought of the possibility of using weapons.*

Embarrassed by his lack of perception, he quickly offered, "If it would make you feel better, I will go collect some."

The princess assured him that it would make her feel much better. Within minutes he returned with two swords, a longbow, and a crossbow with appropriate ammunition.

Jakkon took no time securing horses for himself and the other two in his little group. He chose his favorite, a black mare, and Tanyon's least favorite, a chestnut stallion with a disagreeable disposition. The mare was a sweet ride, but the stallion was a born leader. In fact, he took the leadership role from any rider, which was why he was not a favorite to ride.

Choosing for Kanea was easy because the princess had her own filly, and no one dared question orders from the queen. *The stable hands might want to at least ask me a few questions before they just give me her horse,* Jakkon thought, but he figured that their lack of questioning was because they knew him. If stranger had asked for horse, he was sure that a few questions would have been asked for security's sake. As planned, he met his two companions outside the stable. The elder warrior tossed him the crossbow and the bolts he managed to pick up.

"For the safety of the princess," he said and reached for the black's reins.

"Not that one, Tanyon. I chose your favorite." He smiled his infamous grin that Tanyon hated.

"Oh, no. Not the chestnut," he moaned.

"Something wrong?" Kanea asked when she heard Tanyon. "Absolutely—"

"No, your majesty," Jakkon finished for Tanyon. "Feather-dew here just doesn't like chesties." He laughed and jumped on the mare, while Kanea was rather oblivious to Tanyon's spite toward this certain chestnut. Tanyon, not desiring to seem like a wimp, mounted the resistant animal and began to lead the way. They were ready in time to travel with many of the people going to watch the day's games.

"Safety in numbers," murmured Jakkon.

"Indeed…" Tanyon agreed. "Exactly like I had planned."

"Oh, so you planned for everyone to go out at the same time so then we could use this as a safety measure," Jakkon taunted. Instead of a comeback, he received a glare that spoke of an early death. Kanea was only beginning to realize the antagonistic nature between the two.

"Might we have a pleasant trip without bickering?" requested Kanea. "Anyway, it is not like extreme safety measures are a necessity. Pneutra is very safe."

"If you do not count the Great Wilderness," Jakkon commented. "That relatively unmapped land is only about ten miles south of here, only explored by skilled hunters and woodsmen and riddled with bands of outlaws"

Tanyon's eyes narrowed at the comment. The last thing he wanted was the princess's worrying about getting lost in the Great Wilderness.

Jakkon then rapidly changed the subject. "Why didn't the queen wish to come today?" he inquired.

"She had to settle another dispute between the Kaks and Fays," Kanea explained.

"Not those two farmers again," Tanyon groaned. "How, in one day, could they possibly find something to feud about?!"

"Easily, they're the Kaks and the Fays," Jakkon replied flatly. "They've been feuding since three generations past—all because one sheep wondered into the other's yard, and the dogs killed it."

"Is that how it all happened?" Kanea was impressed that a sentry would be so knowledgeable.

"Yes, though since then they have had other reason for feuding. Your father was an expert at convincing them to stop—not by force, but by diplomacy. I was able to watch him judge them a few years back."

"He was very diplomatic," the princess agreed quietly. Tanyon hinted to Jakkon that he should cut the talk about the late king; his death was still too near for the princess to handle much vocal reminiscing.

Asher and Denel wished to go before the crowd and make some strategy assessments based on the lay of the land. Nicoron, however, did not join them. He lingered around the stable excessively brushing Thundersbane's mane. When people inquired about his lingering, Nic truthfully replied that he was waiting to meet someone before the day's games. His answer satisfied most people. Denel raised a brow, but he respected his friend's privacy.

"Hello," came that musical voice he was waiting to hear.

"Dibla," he replied and tried to smile his most charismatic smile.

"What a charming smile!" she complimented his attempt, and Nic blushed. Had he been more attentive he might have noticed that her comment was rather unusual since no one before had ever said that.

"Will you be at the games today?" he asked after a moment of awkward silence.

"Of course, I would not miss seeing you snatch a trophy from the hands of your opponents," she sang with a coquettish grin.

"I might not take the trophy," he said, trying to be modest.

"Nicoron, you're not a usual nobling. You have what it takes to be the best, and you should only accept being the best." She deftly preened the cocky youth's feathers with additional compliments until it was time for him to leave.

"I will see you at the games," he promised as he mounted his horse.

"Absolutely!" she said as he rode away.

~

Tanyon enjoyed the uneventful ride to the forest stadium. *Nothing exciting, nothing wrong,* he thought with comfort. When the trio arrived, attendants took their horses to the small stable. Tanyon gazed around carefully as they escorted the princess to the royal booth. *Now, now,* he chided himself, *you're in Pneutra, what could possibly happen?*

Jakkon noticed his uneasy manner. "Rather uneasy, are we?" he teased, then smiled. "Do not worry, Tanyon! What could go wrong?"

Tanyon heaved. *Is this guy a mind reader?* "I cannot dislodge this ominous sense. I feel as if we should on our highest guard and be ready to protect the princess at any moment."

Much to his surprise, Jakkon agreed. "We should be very protective of the princess." At the mention of her title, Kanea turned to them from talking to a servant.

"Is something wrong?" she asked when she saw their solemn expressions.

"Of course not, Princess Kanea," Tanyon replied and tried in vain to brighten his somber face.

"Yes, we were merely discussing how to be better prepared for a surprise attack," Jakkon added.

Way to go, Jakkon. Tanyon wanted to grumble. *Just make the princess feel as if she is in the hands of inexperienced trainees-of-war.*

"You really don't think we are in danger of an attack!" she nearly laughed, and Jakkon laughed with her.

"Oh course, not, but you know how Tanyon is just a worry wart." The elder scowled, but Kanea was not really listening.

Tanyon smiled. *At least she didn't hear that wisecrack.*

The royal booth has the best view—great for seeing which contestant is winning! Jakkon thought. The comfortable padded couches only added to the pleasure of the spectacular view. Jakkon mentioned to Tanyon that it might be wise for one of them to sit and one to stand. Tanyon raised a brow. "I thought it would be quite strategic for us both to stand."

A smile crept up on his face, and Jakkon feigned to be terribly upset then recovered.

"But what if someone tried to attack from underneath?" the younger man countered, but Tanyon opined that for someone to bore through the solid wood supporting the booth just to attack the princess was very unlikely. "There are easier ways, so both of us will stand."

The organizer of the games suddenly appeared. "Princess Kanea, the games officially begin in the next ten minutes. I was wondering if you are prepared for the signaling arrow."

"Are my bow and quiver ready?"

"I should hope so," he stuttered then quickly left without saying another word.

"Very good manners," Jak muttered.

"Better than yours," Tanyon snapped back. The organizer again appeared, this time with a case.

"Here are your bow and arrows, Princess." When the organizer left, Jakkon chuckled.

"Remind me never to seek the organizer's position. He looked like he was about to pull out his hair."

"It is not like children are easy to work with," Tanyon stated. "I hear the noblings can be quite the pain."

Kanea turned around in her seat. "I always thought that noblings were very nice."

"Maybe, but you haven't met all the noblings. Ours are quite polite, I assure you, but some are little curs," Jakkon replied.

"Jakkon, shush!" Tanyon scolded. "Some of those 'curs' are skilled in swordsmanship, archery, and every other fighting style. I would guess they would make quick work of you."

Jakkon gave Tanyon a questioning look. "I am a trained

warrior, and they are but children. How could they possibly defeat me in any way?"

"How about the fact that they can afford to have the best tutors in the land train them in all fighting styles."

"Excellent point, Tanyon, but it still doesn't pass the fact that they are children, and I am a man," Jakkon insisted with an arrogant air.

"Some of those children are as old as you," the elder informed the cocky one.

Kanea sought to stop the incessant arguing. "Oh, look it is almost time to start the games!" She pulled out her bow and quiver, awaiting the announcement. Once the announcer stated that the games were beginning, Kanea let fly the arrow. The first games were duels of jousting, which Tanyon thought a rather senseless sport and was bored by watching. First was Dakiel against Langhen, and then Pneutra against Teral, and finally the winners faced off. Jakkon was bored as well but tried not to show his boredom because Kanea was enthralled.

Nicoron waited silently for the hunting competition to be announced.

"You know that hunting is the last competition," Denel said from behind him. "I scouted the surrounding area and discovered that there is a buck with ten layers of antlers." He smiled.

"Whoever gets that one will definitely win," Nicoron returned his wide smile.

"You and Asher really did some scouting? Is that not cheating?"

"Not this time." He laughed. "By the way, why did you stay behind?" Denel had been dying to ask the question since they had last parted ways.

Nicoron hesitated slightly then answered. "Someone wanted to speak their good wishes before I went hunting."

Nic noticed that Denel didn't quite seem satisfied, though he didn't press his friend for any more information.

Chapter Nine

NICORON HEARD A horn blow. Denel recognized the sound and started for the door.

"Hurry!" he admonished. "Asher is about to compete any minute, and he'd be disappointed if you weren't there when he won the competition."

"All right, all right," Nicoron replied, not really appreciating being rushed. He handed Thundersbane's reins to a stable boy before he raced off. Asher was in the boxes, awaiting the call of the princess.

⁓

Tari mounted Prince in the boxes. She proudly wore the teal color of Teral. The boy next to her wore the forest-green color of Pneutra. She heard him whisper, "Ready to win this, Lightning?" The horse snorted in a competitive way.

Tari leaned over. "I guess you're ready for a fight?"

"You bet."

"Good, because Prince and I aren't going to just stand here and *let* you win."

The boy laughed at this boast. "Well, good. I always love a good competition. By the way, I'm Asher."

"I'm Tari, and I like a good competition too."

"Excellent. I guess I shall see you at the end."

"Likewise," Tari responded.

~

"Princess Kanea, it is time to start the jumping games," announced the organizer.

"Very well. Let them begin," Kanea said, trying not to sound so excited she couldn't talk straight. Tanyon leaned forward. How he loved a good horse race. Jakkon examined the horses and riders. He tried to anticipate which team would be most likely to win.

~

The announcer began the countdown until the race. Tari leaned forward and whispered into her horse's ear the words that had been their slogan for as long as they had been a team.

"Go for the gold!"

The blockades were lifted, and Prince leaped forward with his famous beginning start that usually gave them at least a neck-length start, but Asher's steed was scarcely a hand's span behind Prince. *He is faster than I could have ever anticipated!* Tari was taken aback by this realization, but she didn't let the knowledge distract from the race, mainly because the first hurdle was coming.

Prince practically flew over the obstacle with ease. Asher's Lightning did too, but Prince was faster in between hurdles. By the third hurdle of the contest Lightning was falling from Prince's flank. For Prince to take the winning lead early in the game and maintain it was typical; this was their strategy.

Asher, however, had a different game plan; and so far, everything had been going exactly as planned. His strategy was for Lightning to run just fast enough to be second throughout most of the race, thus reserving his energy. Then at the end of the race, they would let loose and pull in front, but Asher hadn't planned on Prince's being quite the runner he was. The rider could feel that Lightning was nearly giving his all in order to remain second. The two horses pulled away from the main group of contestants.

~

Jakkon had appreciated the royal booths view before, but not like he had now. He was practically leaning over the princess watching the bronze steed and black steed leave the other horses in the dust and fight for the finish line. He glanced at Kanea and suppressed a chuckled. Like himself, she was enthralled in the game. Tanyon watched from his standing point. He was impressed by the excellent horsemanship being displayed by the two contestants—surprisingly from Pneutra and Teral.

"I would have thought Dakiel would lead the game," Tanyon thought aloud.

"One would have thought that," Jakkon replied. "but Dakielites dote on their horses. The masterlings pamper their horses with carrots and apples, even sugar."

"Thus making the horses heavy," Kanea added.

"Exactly," Jakkon confirmed. "The other noblings however train their horses for these races."

"You mean that the horses with silver bridles were not expecting?" Tanyon inquired, rather bewildered, for he had never once considered that the bulge around the waist of a Dakielite pony was a sign of overfeeding. Jakkon and Kanea turned and looked at him in a way he did not think very flattering. Fortunately, they refrained from speaking, and his dignity was protected. Attention turned back to the game. The bronze Pneutraite team had exceeded the flank of the Teralian team but was behind by only a neck's length.

~

Tari tried not to concentrate on the fact that Asher was catching up, but on the hurdles before them. Prince never grazed the tip of a hurdle, but this was not exactly racing on trails on the beach from back home. This course required concentrating on the game—not competitors. She checked Prince's impeccable rhythm.

Onlookers would have thought that Prince had been born for jumping the way his hooves were in the strict rhythm whether or not he was racing or jumping. The hurdles became higher each time, and Tari had to remind herself to raise her body higher when Prince jumped. Finally, she saw the last hurdle in sight. Asher did too, and the appearance of the hurdle gave each rider more energy. At Asher's urging, Lightning came neck to neck with Prince. The final hurdle approached, and they lifted off the ground together.

~

Jakkon let out a whoop. It seemed as if Pneutra had won.

"Pneutra has pulled through!" he cheered. Tanyon looked at him strangely.

"We didn't win. I have no doubt that Teral won the jumping contest."

"Was it so?" Kanea questioned. "I thought it was a tie." All three looked at each other with puzzled looks.

"I guess we'll soon find out," Kanea surmised. Apparently, the judge was having difficulty deciding who had won as well. Everyone watched as he went down and asked the contestants themselves.

～

Tari was convinced the run had ended in a tie, and Asher agreed, though there was no way to be completely sure. Tari usually trained her ears to hear the thuds of the horses' hooves when the race was close, but she could not remember this time. Asher was gracious enough to accept a tie. The judge seemed relieved to be able to proclaim a draw, since no one could ever have decided the real winner—if there even was one. Asher and Tari held up the medal together, and the crowds cheered.

Nic could not find a way to express the pride instigated by the amazing horsemanship shown by Asher. Denel was by Nic clapping and hooting the Quariopel way, loud and long. Tari and Asher retreated with their horses to the stable. Tari was holding the gold and blue medal and said to Asher, "You should take this. You and Bronzy did well."

"No," Asher objected. "You and Blackie gave Lightning and me a real challenge."

"Lightning is a good name for a good horse," Tari commented, not really knowing what instigated their small talk.

"Thanks, what is yours? I mean your horse's name?" he asked with a grin.

"Prince." Tari smiled back. He did not seem too bad.

"Prince, that's a strong name for a strong steed," Asher patted Prince's neck. "Is he of Dakielite descent?"

"I don't know," Tari replied.

"You don't know?" Asher seemed very surprised.

"Indeed, I found him as a foal on the beach. He had been abandoned, and I felt sorry for him."

"Who wouldn't?" Asher murmured sympathetically.

"Anyway, I took him home, fed him, and cared for him. When he showed a great talent in jumping, I began training him and here we are." She chuckled. "Actually, we have not truly been defeated until now."

Asher raised a brow. "Really? Well, I am glad that we have been able to challenge you." They laughed together. "Tari, I will be seeing you." He smiled a smile that Tari thought very charming.

"See you around, Asher."

∾

Nic made his way to the stable and caught Asher and Tari parting. He also noticed that Tari was holding the medal. Asher led Lightning his way.

"Good jumping, brother!" he said admiringly.

"Thanks, Nic!" Asher smiled, but Nic guessed his broad smile was not due to his compliment. Teasingly he said, "You do know it is not customary for people to marry people from other cantons, right?" Asher gave him a death look and went on.

Nicoron left to check on Thundersbane. The next competition would be racing, then horse tricks, followed by the hunting. Whoever made it to the finals would compete the next day, and whoever won would carry the title of best rider in Levea.

He knew Dakiel and Teral were favored to win, particularly the triplets of Dakiel and the Helyanwe trio. When he arrived at Thundersbane's stall, he saw a note stuck between the slabs of wood.

Meet me at the Hulder's Clearing at noon.
Dibla

The tiny handwriting denoted a female writer, and the signature was enough for Nic, but then he reminded himself that noon was the time for the hunting game. He groaned inwardly at his conundrum—the Girl or the Game...

Thundersbane snorted as if to show his disapproval at this possible tryst, but Nicoron did not notice. Instead he was intent on figuring out how to make the "Girl or the Game" become the "Girl *and* Game." Suddenly he figured that if he headed for Hulder's Clearing while he was hunting, he could meet her for a few minutes, and then continue hunting. His reasoning seemed plausible, and he settled on his plan.

Kanea scrutinized the racing games. The winners seemed obvious to her but ascertaining the winners of the horse tricks was harder. Kanea was rather bored by the end of the second game and was relieved when the hunters were called in. Hunter and horse lined up, and the gate was opened. At exactly twelve o'clock, each hunter would be released and whoever came back with the best deer, fox, etc. would win the medal.

"Oh, look!" Kanea squealed. "There is Nic!" Tanyon nodded, but Jakkon was surprised by her delight.

"You mean Lordling Nicoron Salindone, son of Lord Nanook Salindone?"

"Yes," Kanea replied, "Nic."

"I didn't know that he had a nickname. I didn't even know he was a hunter."

"He is a fairly good hunter," Tanyon whispered in his ear.

"But why does Kanea call him Nic?"

"He is her personal guard," Tanyon whispered back.

"Oh," Jakkon sounded a bit down, "She never calls me by my nickname."

"Probably because you don't have one."

"Yes, I do!" Jakkon retorted, trying not to interrupt the princess' interest.

"Very, well, then maybe it's because she doesn't know it!" Tanyon whispered fiercely.

"I must remedy that," Jakkon surmised.

"Jakkon! She is the princess. It would not be appropriate!" Tanyon scolded severely. "What is your nickname?" Much to his dismay, Jakkon refused to answer his question. *One would think a warrior would have more scruples!* he told himself.

Nicoron's main priority was to make it to Hulder's Clearing as fast as he could so as to ensure that he could have time for hunting. The designated rendezvous was somewhat farther from the arena than Nic would have preferred, but for a pretty girl he reasoned the detour was worth it. He arrived there within ten minutes and was surprised to see no one waiting.

"Dibla?" he called.

"I am here, Nicoron," came the beautiful voice from above. Dibla leaped to the ground from a low branch.

"Why were you up there?" Nic asked.

"Have you not heard? Horrible wolf-like creatures have been roaming in the shadows. I thought that being in a branch would be some sort of protection."

Nicoron chuckled at the childish fear Dibla showed. "Do not fear. If any monster came to harm you, I would be here."

"I know you would," Dibla smiled and slipped her arm through his. Nic blushed slightly. "But I am not as afraid as I seem," she replied. Suddenly her sweet smile faded, and a face of cold stone seemed to take place.

"I didn't mean to seem as if I were underestimating your abilities. I only meant to offer you my services if needed." Nic was confused at her sudden change in demeanor. She smiled again, but not with the sweet one that had its place before. She pulled away and turned to face him directly.

"I gladly accept your offer," she said with her cold smile, making him feel rather uncomfortable.

He heard the sound of thuds behind him, but before he could turn to see who or what was coming, pain and darkness enveloped him. The last thing he remembered was Dibla and her stony face.

Chapter Ten

IT WAS THE third day of the Nobling Duels, Archer Day. The Helyanwe trio, however, would not competing until the end of the day, after the annual competition with the triplets of Dakiel. Strangely, a hunting contestant had disappeared the day before during the noon hunt. A search had continued all night, but nothing ever came of the hunt.

Nicoron Salindone became the discussion of the citadel once again—but not because of his swordsmanship. His disappearance puzzled many, but a consistent search could not be completed for the nights had been dangerous with the strange, fur-covered creatures that made few appearances on the far outskirts of the citadel limits.

Nicoron awakened. His cold body ached, and his wrists and ankles were aching. *How long have I been asleep?* he wondered. When he finally forced open his eyes, he saw only darkness, but then he noticed a faint light to his left.

When he tried to move toward the light, he could not. A clanking sound spoke to him of chains. *Chains?* he wondered. He tried to move again. Sudden realization came. *I am chained to a tree!* He began to look around him in greater earnest. The light, which was a campfire, was surrounded by men in dark suits. He called to them.

"What do you want?" grumbled a bulky one.

"Where am I? Why do you have me chained?" he demanded of his captors, but the man refused to answer. He tried to examine his surroundings in the darkness of the night. He heard something of a growl.

"Hello," said one of the men sitting around the fire. "Looks like one of the Crak-wolves is hungry."

"Feed that chained brat to them," suggested another.

"No, the princess needs him," replied the bulky one.

Who is the princess of whom they are speaking? It surely cannot be Kanea!

"Do we have to do *everything* Princess Dibla says?" retaliated the other.

Nic gasped a barely audible gasp. *Dibla?! Could they be talking about my Dibla. Surely it cannot be her either!* Deep down in Nic's innermost being, his instincts told him that the Dibla he had met the past day was the one about whom they were talking. Then a whistle was sounded, and one of the men whistled back. Something landed nearby.

"Have you Crakaton soldiers been behaving yourselves?" came that musical voice Nic had thought he adored.

"Of course, your majestic majesty," replied one of the men with a gallant bow. If Nic had been able to see the withering look Dibla gave the man, he would have laughed. His eyes wandered to the huge beast beside her, and he gasped. The beast appeared to be a dragon—like the ones he had seen in drawings in a book. When the beast rose to stand, its head was within a few yards of the tree's canopy. The dragon was predominantly angular and long, with the exception of its hind thighs, which were about a yard's width. Small horns protrusions followed the animal's backbone down its spine to the tip of the tail. Longer horns were on the dragon's forehead, and smaller ones protruded from its chin. The tail itself was unique because it spiraled in a strange way.

Dibla turned to Nicoron and smiled her cold smile. "And how is our guest?" she asked as she took some of her very articulated steps toward him.

Nic grimaced. "Could not be better," he snapped.

"Oh, good." She clasped her hands.

"I am curious though."

"Oh?"

"Indeed, why am I here?" he demanded.

"Oh, that…" She chuckled. "My father wants to meet you."

"I guess that would be flattering if I were not chained to a tree."

"My father can scare people sometimes."

"Like your scaly pet?"

"Just like Screecher." Dibla smiled.

"Screecher? Some name," Nicoron commented.

"I know. It fits him perfectly," Dibla boasted. She waved her hand, and the dragon emitted a howling screech. The lordling wished his hands were not chained so he could cover his ears.

"Perfectly," Nic echoed quietly.

~

The trio was standing in front of the citadel's stables discussing the previous day. The city was bustling. News about the Nobling Duels and a lordling's disappearance was enough to keep the murmuring constant. Tari's attention was drawn to the horses trotting through the streets. From their appearance, she could gather they had been riding all morning, probably searching for Nicoron since dawn. She saw Asher and another sturdy nobling riding side by side. Asher was hanging his head as he dismounted. She approached him from behind.

"Asher…" He whirled to see who it was.

"Tari, what are you doing here?"

"Waiting for the sun dial to turn to seven o'clock," she replied. "What about you?"

"Just returned from a search. Lightning needs a rest." He sighed. "I just wish we could find Nic."

"Was he a relative?" she ventured to ask.

"My brother," Asher whispered.

Tari could have kicked herself. "I am sorry; I should not have asked," she apologized, but Asher didn't seem to mind.

"I just wish we could find him. I know he could take care of himself, but I have this horrible feeling that something awful has happened to him."

Tari tried to be sympathetic, but these situations didn't show her shining moments. She tried to change the subject. "Would you like to come and watch our game today?" she asked hesitantly.

"You are in the archery?"

"No, I mean, my sisters are, and we are a part of the final

cross-country competition," she explained. "We face the triplets of Dakiel—Astair, Astar, and Aster."

Asher chuckled. "I hear they are the immature ones."

"Indeed." Tari rolled her eyes, and then timidly asked again.

Asher thought for a minute. "All right," he finally said and smiled that charming smile of his.

Tari smiled in return. "See you then."

Tanyon paced in front of the princess' door, waiting for Kanea. Jakkon was leaning against the wall.

"Why are you pacing, Tanyon?" Jakkon asked.

"I am worried about Lordling Nicoron," he replied.

"I think that an experienced lordling can take care of himself," Jakkon mused.

"That is it," Tanyon pointed out. "Lordling Nic is experienced. He knows these woods like he would know his own. He couldn't have gotten lost, and if he got distracted while hunting he would have been back by now. Unless—"

"Unless some fire-breathing dragon swept him up to a cave high up on a cliff for lunch!" Jakkon's imagination was soaring.

Tanyon moaned. "Dragons no longer exist!" He sighed. "I was going to say unless something bad happened to him."

"I was close," Jakkon grumbled. Right then Kanea came out of her room, wearing her hunting uniform and carrying her archery set.

"All ready," she said. "I would like to attend the cross-country today. Have you readied the horses?"

Tanyon stepped up. "Yes, indeed, your highness," he said

and grinned mischievously at Jakkon. The other gulped, making Tanyon smile with satisfaction. *I will not be the one riding a stubborn stallion today.* He led the way to stables where the stable boys had their horses all ready. Then it was the trek to the woodland arena. Other than Jakkon's trying to control the stubborn chestnut, there was nothing of amusement. Finally, the trio arrived and were seated in the royal booth.

Jakkon had found it difficult to control the horse he had been assigned. The chestnut pulled to the right when his rider needed to go to the left and to the left when he need to go right. Fortunately, the horse at least followed the crowd of humans and horses. Jakkon arrived with the others in spite of the degree of difficulty involved.

When they reached the royal booth, Tanyon beheld two chairs behind the royal couch. Assuming they were for the guards, he took a seat.

"Is Tanyon asleep already?" Kanea asked when she looked over to see the elder warrior snoring. Jakkon burst into laughter and was quickly silenced by the princess. Tanyon was indeed sleeping.

"I think he was one of the volunteers who searched for Lordling Nicoron last night," Jakkon informed the princess while trying to withhold his chuckles.

Kanea sobered. "Poor Nic!" she nearly sobbed.

Jakkon ventured into the unknown. "Were you close?"

"Close friends, but nothing more. After all, he was my royal guard," Kanea replied.

"Oh, I see," Jakkon mumbled.

Chapter Eleven

ACCORDING TO THE Pneutraite sundial, the time was seven-thirty as Tari watched the final "Horsey Day" race begin. Kaete was astride her bay mare, awaiting the starting signal as was Astar, her opponent. According to plan, Kaete would start the race as the first rider, then pass the baton to Lura, and finally to Tari. The youngest was not only the lightest rider but owned the fastest horse of the three.

"Bring the fastest last" was what their father had admonished them years ago, and they followed his advice.

Kanea had retrieved her bow and quiver so she could signal the beginning of the last game. The princess did not even wait for the organizer to finish telling her that the contestants were ready. Twang! The arrow soared high into the air and hit the target. Jakkon watched the two horses speed out of the arena.

"Cross-country horse racing was always one of my favorite steed competitions," he stated.

"Oh, really?" Kanea turned to face him. "I really have never understood it."

"Oh, the competition is very exhilarating!"

"Could you explain it to me?" she asked.

"Of course!" Jakkon felt honored that he would be selected to explain such an exciting race to the princess. "Cross-country racing requires much skill and speed, on both the rider and the horse's part. A path through the woods is constructed so that it circles back to the arena. Obstacles such as muddy patches and stacks of wood or stone are strategically placed to add obstacles the rider and horse must dodge or hurdle. The planners also make use the lay of the land. Places with sloping and uneven ground are also included in the path."

"But what does all this have to do with the game?" the princess interrupted.

"Being able to maneuver this course shows the skill of the horse and rider. Whoever can complete the track first without cheating is obviously the best team. This race is done in relay style. Each team is given a baton, and the first contestant carries it through his or her section of the course and passes it on to the next and so on. The very last of the team to compete has the job of handing the baton to the judge, and whichever team get to him first wins," Jakkon explained patiently.

"That race does sounds like a lot of fun!" she squealed in excitement. "Have you ever been in a race like that?"

The warrior cleared his throat nervously. "Well, not exactly. I did not have many playmates as a child, and I often played or read alone. Most of what I know, I know from reading." He was usually ashamed of not having the experience of an average warrior.

The princess was still impressed, however. "I have not met a warrior who reads," she said. "Most only care about fighting."

Jakkon cleared his throat and blushed ever so slightly. "I found reading in the library very much enjoyable. How about you?"

"Oh, I love reading. History is my favorite subject. What is your favorite?"

"I like science; biology is my specialty I would like to think. Studying the different kinds of animals is quite interesting. Then the different kinds of dogs or horses! Exhilarating!" Jakkon's ardent love for the sciences made Kanea chuckle a little. The thuds of hooves made them turn. The Teralian rider had completed her round with the Dakiel rider close behind.

Tari shouted an encouraging comment to Lura as she grabbed the baton from Kaete and raced off. Aster started about thirty seconds later. Kaete breathed heavily.

"The track is difficult," she noted, "but I think Lura can handle it though."

"Was Astar keeping up with you?"

"He stayed behind me for the whole run. I think he fed his horse too much." The sisters chuckled together.

"Probably," Tari agreed, then she sobered. "But it still looks like the Dakiel triplets are using some strategy. If you noticed, they are saving Astair for the last, and he is their fastest rider."

"But so are you," Kaete assured her. "You have the fastest horse, and you are the lightest, most adept rider of us three. You have a winning chance." She patted Prince's neck. Tari accepted her sister's encouragement with a big smile.

"I think you can win too," came a favorable-sounding voice from behind.

The sisters turned to see who was talking. "Asher, you did come!"

"And how do you two know each other?" Kaete asked.

"We competed yesterday in the jumping contest," he explained.

"We also were tied," Tari added, and her eldest sister nodded and smiled slightly.

"So Prince finally met his match, I guess. What is your horse's name?"

"Lightning," Asher replied.

"Sounds like a horse to match Prince," Kaete approved. "And why are you here?" Tari thought that her question was rather dumb.

"I promised Tari I would watch her game," he replied with his charming smile. Kaete nodded. He turned to Tari.

"I'll see you win then, Tari."

"See you around, Asher." She turned and watched him head to the stands. Kaete leaned over Tari's shoulder.

"Nice catch, but for people to marry people from other cantons is still very uncommon."

"Kaete, stop it!"

～

"Hmm, it looks like it will be a close race," Jakkon commented. "See how the last two riders came in so close."

"Close competition is always the best," the princess remarked.

"I agree."

Silence settled between them, and the minutes passed by.

Jakkon did not know how to resume conversation, and the awkward silence loomed like an unwanted storm cloud.

Kanea did not feel the shadowy silence; instead, she was wondering why the organizer didn't organize entertainment for the intermittent times when the contestants were racing through the woods. *Jakkon will probably know,* she thought.

Tanyon snorted and slowly opened his eyes. When he realized that he had fallen asleep right in front of Jakkon and the princess, he sat up and tried to act dignified. *That's ruined,* said his realistic side. He could hear his companions snickering behind him. "Uh, who's winning?" He tried to draw attention away from himself since his neck and face were turning red.

"The Teralian team came through fastest in the first round," the princess replied.

"What round is being run now?"

"The second."

"Great, I only missed one third of it," he mumbled to himself. At that moment Lura streaked in on her steed.

"Oh, almost two thirds!" he moaned again. Before the Teralian rider could hand over the baton, the Dakielite rider skidded into the arena.

◊

Tari was on Prince ready for Lura. She glanced toward the stadium, hoping she could find Asher, but she couldn't see him. Her middle sister pulled up beside her and handed her the baton. As soon as Tari felt the wood in her hand, she and Prince galloped out of the arena. Prince's muscles rippled underneath her as he leaped forward. The nobling could hear Astair on his purebred Dakielite horse behind her. She took care to pay attention to the track, so she wouldn't go off it. The track began with a normal running track, but eventually the pathway became rocky and rough. Then came the obstacles. A log that had been placed across the road, and a rock that had been set in the middle of the track were merely the beginning. Prince cleared these with such ease that Tari thought she could hear him laughing at them, but both the rider and the horse knew that the trail was to become much more difficult.

Astair was keeping good time and was actually reducing the distance between them. Even though to look back was tempting, she refused to hazard a glimpse. She knew that simply taking that glance could affect Prince's gait.

The trail turned sharply to the right and then to the left. In addition to these turns, large rocks were in the way. Tari knew the point of this placement was to prove the maneuvering abilities of the horse and rider. Jumping the boulders would be the first idea to come to the head of a rider but doing so would run the risk of leaving the track. She signaled for Prince to slow ever so slightly. The steed practically danced around the rocks, while Astair's horse had to slow to a trot behind them.

Climbing a hill immediately followed these obstacles. The rough hill was the halfway mark, and after descending the hill, the trail would curve back to the arena. Tari elevated herself in the saddle as they came down the hill. Next was a muddy trail dotted with rocks. Prince was a good ride on mud, but she heard Astair's slip on one point. After that lengthy stretch were higher and thicker logs to jump, and the nobling could feel that

Prince did not take these with as much ease as the earlier obstacles. She smiled as they approached a rather steep slope. The competition was coming to an end!

~

Tanyon remained quiet while the princess and his fellow warrior discussed the past winners of races. He never cared so much for statistics, champions, or thing of the like. He would rather train himself or work with his trainees-of-war. Dueling was another delightful pastime of his—not fatal, of course. His mind wandered to Nicoron's disappearance. He knew Nic well from the past few years of their service to the queen. He might have even been brave enough to call him a friend. Tanyon was truly worried about this sudden vanishing. His thoughts were interrupted by his companions' mirthful laughter.

"What is funny?" he asked.

"Jakkon was just telling the most hilarious story. Tell it again, Jakkon! Please…" requested Kanea.

"It would be my pleasure, Princess Ilindel." The younger replied with a bow. "It goes like this—" But Tanyon did not hear. His attention was captured by a dark object on the horizon that looked large and seemed to be flying.

"What is that?" he mused aloud, completely missing the punchline as he pointed.

"Aren't you paying any attention to my tale?" Jakkon asked with exasperation.

"Don't you see that dark object in the sky?" Tanyon asked as he continued to point.

"What dark object?"

"I saw it too," the princess interjected, "but I do not see it any longer."

Jakkon said, "It was probably just the normal affect of staring at the sun too long. Perfectly explainable, scientific, and normal," he muttered. About that time, they heard the faint thud of hooves.

"Oh, here come the last pair!" Kanea squealed with sudden excitement.

~

Tari spotted the woodland arena as the trails began to widen. She could also perceive that Astair was encouraging his steed to go faster. Soon they were running neck to neck. Prince galloped as fast as he could, but his opponent was catching up to him. They entered the arena, and eldest of the Dakiel triplets was becoming faster than they were. Tari encouraged Prince forward, but he could not go any faster. A sinking feeling settled in the dukeling's insides as she began to realize that Prince might not be able to win this time.

~

"Teral does not look really good," Jakkon stated. "See how Dakiel is making the lead."

Though Tanyon nodded his assent, his mind was not with the game; it was with Nic and the dark object in the sky. He had seen the spots that were the result of staring at the sun before, and what he had seen was nothing like them.

Kanea cried out in surprise, which caused Tanyon to look up. He smiled.

~

It was nearing the end, and Tari was beginning to accept the fact that she would not win this time, but suddenly Prince lurched forward. She was caught off guard at this unexpected rapidity. They went from neck to neck to a neck's length ahead. Tari hardly knew when she and Prince had passed the judges. The horse skidded to a stop and reared in triumph. They had won! The dukeling whooped and stood up in the saddle.

Jakkon stood in awe and felt like laughing. He had underestimated the Teralian team. Tanyon clapped. "That was quite a good race, even though I was only awake for one third of it." He made a joke of himself—something he rarely did. This joking signified his good mood.

Kanea was very impressed and found herself speechless. She satisfied herself with clapping with Tanyon and the rest of the audience. The dukeling stood in the saddle and waved her arms. Kanea laughed.

"She sure is enthusiastic," Jakkon commented.

"Wouldn't you be excited if you just won the grand competition of cross-country?" Tanyon retorted.

"Good point."

Tari handed the baton to the judge. Smiling, the judge placed the medal over her head and proclaimed her the winner. Astair was panting as he slipped of his lathered horse. Tari's sisters and many others, including Asher, rushed into the arena to extend their congratulations. Asher wrapped his arm around her shoulder and patted her on the back.

"You were amazing," he said admiringly.

"You did not even see Prince in action," she retorted.

"No, but you came in first, and that is what matters most. Of course, it doesn't if you cheated."

"Excuse me!" she lightly punched him in the shoulder.

"I was only jesting!" He pulled back in defense and smiled charmingly.

"I know, but you're too much fun to tease," Tari replied with a smile.

Kaete and Lura winked at each other as they listened, but Tari and Asher did not notice their sisterly signal.

Chapter Twelve

ABOUT AN HOUR later, Kanea was patting the neck of her filly. She reminisced about the past hour. She had had a wonderful time watching the race, even though most of the race she did not get to see. *I think I made a good trade—archery for horse racing. Now I can go and watch the finals,* she thought.

"Are you ready, your highness?" Tanyon asked from his chestnut mount. Jakkon had usurped the black pony again, and now the elder warrior was not in such a good mood.

"Yes, Tanyon, lead the way," she waved her hand toward the exit door of the stables. Tanyon took the lead, and Jakkon brought up the rear.

∽

Tari had offered for Asher to ride with them back to the citadel. He gladly accepted.

"Good," Kaete said. "I have wanted to meet Lightning."

"Who is Lightning?" Lura asked.

"The horse that almost beat Prince."

"Indeed, that is a horse I would like to meet," the middle sister agreed.

The four of them rode toward the Pneutra capital, allowing the horse to meander for Prince's sake. The delay also gave them time to discuss matters that noblings enjoyed discussing. The Nobling Games premiered in the conversation—like it did in most conversations around this time. Tari gazed around. Woods and forest were all the eye could examine. For the moment, it was peaceful. *Almost too peaceful,* Tari thought. The wind blew softly, and the scent of sweet greenery and smoke filled her nostrils. *Smoke?* the girl wondered, now alarmed.

"Do any of you smell smoke?" she asked her companions. Everyone reined their horse to a stop. Asher sniffed the air and frowned. "Smoke is never a good sign."

"Is it a forest fire?" Kaete inquired.

"Possibly…" he answered.

"Just hold on a second!" Lura interjected. "This is not the time for forest fires. This is fall, and wildfires usually begin in the summer."

"Occasionally they can occur in the early fall," the lordling added. "We had better move faster."

The two warriors also sensed the presence of smoke. They encouraged their horses from a trot to a slow canter. Kanea was slightly worried. "Will we make it to the city in time?" she asked nervously.

"Yes, your highness," Tanyon assured her. "I promise you that we will ensure that you arrive at the citadel safe and sound."

The princess was comforted a little by his assurance. *Oh, stop worrying,* she chided herself. *You are in the hands of two capable warriors. What could possibly go wrong?* Her thoughts were rudely interrupted by the shout of a man coming quickly from behind them.

"Run!" he shouted. Confused she looked about. *What was there to run from?* Suddenly a noise like nothing which Kanea had ever heard reverberated through the woods. Later she described the sound as an extremely high-pitched screech. Jakkon, who fancied himself as having a way with words, said that the sound was like scraping a rusty sword along the ground. Her horse reared and bolted—but not for the sound.

"Tanyon, ride!" commanded Jakkon from behind her. Tanyon glanced back and saw a horrific sight. A beast of strange figure was howling toward them. The two warriors urged their horses to follow Kanea's uncontrollable animal.

When the screech came to the ears of Prince, he literally screamed. Tari was nearly shaken from the saddle as he raced off the road and into the forest. Her sisters called after her, "Tari, hold on!"

Kaete spurred her horse into pursuit of her youngest sister. The other two followed. Tari was confused by her horse's behavior. In all the years of training her beautiful horse, she had never seen him in such a state of panic. Prince had never been spooked by anything, yet now he had fled at the terrifying screech. Now she could not control him in the slightest. Prince galloped through the forest at a speed she had never before experienced. The panicked girl forgot everything but focusing on staying on her horse without getting slapped in the face by branches or swept off by low-hanging limbs.

A movement in the corner of her eye caught her attention. She barely turned her head to see a creature racing parallel to Prince. She could not fully examine what it was for the trees were mere blurs. Suddenly the creature leaped from its flanking course to land directly in front of Prince. The steed reared, pawing the air and trumpeting his anger.

Tari's mouth fell open in awe at the huge creature with a body structure of a wolf. However, this animal was unlike any wolf of Pneutra. The formidable creature barred its monstrous teeth as saliva dripped from its jaws. Its snout was rippled, and its eyes were shaped like a cat's. Its paws were the circumference of a young tree with claws the size of a stiletto dagger. Muscles rippled through the massive, striped body; yet the characteristic that stood out to Tari was the thing's yard-long tail that was bare of fur. The rest of the body was furry like a cat of the mountains. The most striking characteristic was the coloration—black, jagged stripes down its sides from its nose to its tail. Prince stared the massive creature in the eyes, and the creature stared back. The horse could no longer take the watch of the slits and began to run again.

The Crakaton wolf

The creature chased them again. Tari hazarded a brief look back and was mortified that the creature pursuing them did not appear to be struggling to keep up with them.

～

Kanea looked wildly about her. The poor filly was spooked out of her wits and had resorted to the only form of escape that she knew—running away. Tanyon flanked her on the left while Jakkon flanked her right.

"Tanyon," called Jakkon, "look up!"

When Tanyon hazarded a quick look, he saw a terrible sight. In the sky was a dark object that was now closer than it had been earlier that day. The object was long, thin and scaly.

"I knew that wasn't the effect of staring at the sun," Tanyon muttered.

"What is that *thing*?" Kanea asked.

"If I were to guess, I would say a dragon," Jakkon replied.

Kanea thought of her dragon-hide boots and how she was wearing them that day. *Is this dragon coming back for revenge?* she wondered.

"Wait, is someone on that thing?" Jakkon's question caused Kanea to look up.

"I do not care," Tanyon responded. "We need get back to the citadel now!"

"Not going to happen, Tanyon," the younger said. "Look behind you."

Tanyon thought he sounded so calm, but when he turned around, he understood that he misunderstood. The reason the filly had bolted was because a strange wolf-like creature had appeared from the bushes. Now that creature was following them with reinforcements.

~

Tanyon and Jakkon tried to keep the monsters at bay. The crossbow Jakkon possessed proved very useful at discouraging the beasts. Every so often, he would turn in his saddle and expertly launch a bolt at the pursuing creatures; unfortunately, they kept coming.

Tanyon was awed by the endurance of their horses who kept running for hours on end. Eventually, the steeds began to slow down, then they slowed to a halt.

"Tanyon, the horses have stopped," Jakkon said. "We need to fight on the ground."

"Then so be it," Tanyon replied as he slipped off his horse and unsheathed his sword and brandished it. Jakkon followed Tanyon's lead. The horses and Kanea assumed positions behind the two warriors. Two creatures bounded from the bushes and snarled at the trio. Tanyon attacked one, and Jakkon took the other. A furious skirmish arose. Tanyon jabbed his sword into the neck of one, but then another rose to take his place.

Jakkon lunged with his knife into the monster's forehead, and another leaped over the dead body knocking the archer down. In a sudden moment, the creatures stopped attacking them and retreated into the bushes. Tanyon heard a strong howl in the distance preceding the retreat of their pursuers.

"We scared them away!" Jakkon shouted and raised his sword in triumph.

"No, we did not," Tanyon realized. "They were called away. Did you not hear those howls? They sound exactly like the hunting dogs that lords sometimes use to hunt rabbits and foxes. When the lead dog has caught the prey, he howls; and his team responds. Those things did something similar."

"Do you think they could be part of the canine family?" Jakkon asked.

"Right now, I could care less," Tanyon turned to the princess. "How are you?"

The princess gulped. "I—I think I am fine—just exhausted."

"We should return," Jakkon suggested. He tried to mount his horse, but the usually compliant mare walked away from him and laid down in the grass. The other horses followed suit.

"They won't let us ride them!" Kanea despaired.

Tanyon thought for a moment. "If the horses won't allow us to ride them, then we have no way to get home."

"Brilliant, genius," Jakkon muttered. "How long did it take for you to figure that out?"

Tanyon replied with a growl. "I think we should stay here until the horses are rested."

"Those creatures could come back at any moment. I think we should begin our journey back to the citadel. The sooner we return the better."

"I agree, but we have no way back unless we walk, and personally I am too tired to walk," Tanyon retorted.

"So am I," the princess agreed weakly.

"What if they return?" Jakkon countered.

"You and I will fend them off," Tanyon stated. "Protecting

the princess is our main priority."

"Returning the princess to the citadel tonight is also a priority!" Jakkon returned.

"But that is not possible right now. Our horses are tired, we are tired, and even if we could ride, we couldn't reach the citadel before nightfall," Tanyon tried to reason with the upstart.

Kanea decided the time had come for royalty to step in and end the contentious discussion. "I believe Tanyon is right. We cannot return now; our best bet is to rest for a while, perhaps even spend the night, then return."

Tanyon and Jakkon gave their cloaks to Kanea to sleep on. They agreed that they should do everything in their power to make their princess comfortable. Kanea was touched by their efforts, but comfort was out of the equation. Princess Ilindel was accustomed to sleeping on feather mattresses with down pillows and rabbit-fur blankets. *It is going to be a long, weary night.*

Chapter Thirteen

KAETE, LURA, AND Asher had lost sight of Tari, but they continued to follow her trail. Both sisters were extremely worried for their beloved younger sister.

Asher sympathized with the sisters; after all, both families had lost a sibling within forty-eight hours. His mind began to work. *Is this some sort of pattern? Are there sibling snatchers hiding in the woods?* He shook his head to rid himself of the ridiculous thoughts.

The trio easily found the trail of trampled grass Prince had left which served as their guide. On and on they went until night had nearly fallen.

"To go on any longer is not safe," Asher stated. "We should turn back while there is yet light."

"We cannot go back without Tari," Lura exploded.

"Trust me, I do understand your feelings. My brother is still missing from yesterday," he added in a remorseful tone. Lura's expression softened slightly as he continued. "But we will do neither of them any good if we are lost in these woods as well."

"How can we get back?" Kaete asked. She was clearly clueless as to where they were.

"I know the way back to the citadel," Asher assured them.

"Follow me." He neck-reined Lightning around and led the sisters back to the safety of the gates.

~

The citadel of Pneutra was in more confusion the next morning than it had ever been. Warriors were being paired and sent out in search of the missing princess and dukeling—not to mention the two warriors. Asher, Denel, and Lord Nanook insisted on returning to the saddles and scouring the forests. The captain of the citadel accepted his unpleasant duty of telling the queen that Princess Kanea had disappeared after being attacked by horrifying creatures—perhaps the same that had slain King Rigal.

When the queen heard the news, it was being said that she had a complete breakdown. Asher could understand why. His queen had lost her husband only a short time ago, and now her only daughter disappeared. Lightning jumped a little.

"You're right, friend. We need to get on," Asher patted his neck affectionately.

"Asher, that is not what he was bucking at," Lord Nanook exclaimed and pointed ahead. Some warriors were leading in an exhausted gray horse.

"Thundersbane!" Asher called out. The silvery stallion's ears perked up at this voice, and the horse bobbed his head. "Father, maybe he can lead us to Nic!"

"Ash, he is too tired to lead anyone anywhere," Denel said. "Let's just get going and not lose any more daylight. My innards are giving me a horrible feeling."

"Your innards?" Nanook raised a brow.

"Sorry, that is warrior talk—not nobling talk."

"Innards?" Asher scrunched his nose. "Gross."

∽

Tari's eyes fluttered open. She felt muscles she had never realized existed, and her body was so sore. She could only tell that it was bright, yet shadowy. Everything else was blurred. The scent of moist soil filled her nose. Something thudded beside her and nudged her gently.

"Prince," she whispered and sat up. Her back was stiff, and she found it rather difficult to sit up. Looking around, she realized she was tucked in between the large roots of a mossy tree. Even though her legs felt as if they had been running for hours, she managed to stand up. Her horse stood next to her, allowing her to lean on him. Tari then recalled everything that had happened the day before.

She and Prince had been chased by a furry, wolf-like creature until evening, when it had suddenly turned around and vanished into the bushes. By then both rider and horse had been exhausted; they literally fell to the ground asleep. Tari now found herself confronted with several problems. They were lost, and she had no idea how to return to the citadel. She had no water or food. That they were in unknown territory that was possibly crawling with giant wolves ready to snatch them up at a moment's notice was foremost on her mind. "We are not in the best of situations, Prince."

As if Prince could understand her words, the horse neighed in agreement. The ready law for when one was lost was for the person to stay in his or her position until found. Tari knew this rule, but she had not had any food or water since the previous morning. *What is the point of obeying the law if you face the possibility of dying before someone finds you?* The dukeling took this matter into consideration and decided to move on until she could find some sort of water source.

"Sorry, boy," she said, "but I need to ride you." Without complaint, the noble steed allowed his rider on his back.

"I do not think we will have to go that far," she mused aloud. "See how the ground is soft? It might be a sign of a nearby spring."

⁓

Morning came and Jakkon, who had the second watch, awoke the other two.

"Morning, yet not *good* morning," he said.

"What is that supposed to mean?" grumbled Tanyon, who was then wishing he had spent the night in his heather cot.

"It means that it is morning, but I will not say what is not."

"You make no sense."

"I mean that I will not say good morning when I do not know if it is a good morning!" exploded Jakkon.

"Soldiers, we have enough trouble on our hands. Do not start bickering again," Kanea admonished them with firmness. "Now, how are we going home?" she proposed the question that had been on the minds of the trio.

Tanyon smiled and extracted a lodestone from his utility belt. "With this, your highness. We will ride our horses, and this glass case with a small gray stone suspended on a pin in it; thus this lodestone like sailors use will guide us," he explained.

Kanea immediately accepted his solution, and Jakkon had no choice but to follow. Though they were thirsty and hungry, they ignored the discomfort with the hope that they would arrive home soon.

～

Dibla and her party stayed in the area two nights. She did not anticipate that kidnapping Nicoron would be so easy and had originally planned for at least two days to accomplish the kidnapping and the terrorizing. Nevertheless, the ease was very much welcomed.

Nicoron's night was the most uncomfortable one of all. His chained arms were irritated, his back was aching, and his legs were sore. In the morning, he was rudely interrupted by one of the guards the Crakaton princess had assigned. One of his hands was unchained so he could eat and drink something that could hardly be called breakfast. Longingly, he gazed at the one he had thought was such a sweet, young lady. She had a whole bed laid out for her and practically a feast had been prepared. Dibla lightly dabbed her lips and gave orders to several of her henchmen. Then she sauntered toward her prisoner.

"Good morning," she greeted in her sweet voice.

"What do you really want with me?" He inquired in an embittered tone of voice.

"I told you last night that my father would like to meet you."

"And who is *he*?" he added jokingly. "The royal king of Crakaton?"

She smiled in a way that did not encourage him. "Why yes!

I know an intelligent lordling when I see one," she replied with such sincerity that Nic found it hard to tell whether or not she was jesting.

"But Crakaton is a barren waste," he protested. "No one could ever live there!"

"Oh, you would be quite surprised," she sneered. Turning with a majestic flair, she commanded her men. "Put him on a Crakaton wolf."

"Which kind?" inquired the large man.

"A smaller one. I would like to save the bulky ones for chasing away trackers," Dibla replied.

Nic was unchained from the tree and loaded like a sack of potatoes onto a hairy, smelly beast. The Crakaton wolf, as Dibla had referred to the animal, growled and stomped its huge paw.

"I know," said the burly man to the creature. "I wouldn't like a cocky nobling on my back either, but Princess Dibla has to have her way."

Nicoron was astounded that the creature calmed at the very mention of Dibla's name.

❧

Tanyon, Kanea, and Jakkon rode in single file through the woods. Tanyon took the lead, relying greatly on his lodestone. Jakkon merely pondered their path, having some doubt about Tanyon and his lodestone. However, he would not cross his fellow soldier, mainly because Kanea approved of Tanyon's idea. Still he wished they had traveled the previous night and had followed the stars.

Kanea was loving the scenery—the trees, the dead leaves

that crunched underneath her horse, and everything appeared almost magical right now. The sun was shining through the canopy, making the morning dew glisten like the jewels of Langhen. The trees that overshadowed their path offered some shade from the bright sun. Leaves drifted from the trees, reminding the princess of Pneutra that fall was now in full force. She sighed barely audibly. A chilly autumn breeze whisked through the trees, and she shivered.

"Do you need a cloak, your highness?" offered Jakkon from behind her. He had already begun to take his off.

"Thank you, Jakkon, but I will be fine," the princess insisted and pulled her own cloak closer around her.

∿

Tari rode Prince for most of the morning. She soon began to tire of the constant riding, but Prince still had firing energy in him. Tari tried singing to keep her hopes and spirits alive but having never been truly alone before made it hard for her to remain optimistic. She finally settled on humming an old hunting tune to keep up her spirits. Verse one passed and so did verse two. She was about to begin verse three when a sound came from the bushes ahead of her.

"Whoa, boy," she whispered to Prince. The horse obeyed.

∿

Suddenly, Tanyon's horse stopped, sniffed the air, and then lunged forward. The other animals reacted so quickly that the riders would have barely noticed anything changing—until the lunge, of course.

"Tanyon, where are you going?" Kanea shouted after him.

Her mount must have been trained to follow the lead horse because the mare also lunged forward. Jakkon spurred his horse into following.

~

Tari nearly screamed when a man on a horse cantered up to her. Tanyon was bewildered to find a young girl on a black horse standing in front of him. Behind him came Princess Kanea. Tari was rather dumbfounded at this unexpected occurrence.

"Who are you?" Tari asked.

Tanyon replied, "I am Tanyon Fitherlew, protector of her highness Princess Kanea. Now who are you?"

"Tari Helyanwe, dukeling," the girl responded though a tad timidly.

"How did you get way out here?" Princess Kanea asked.

"I was chased by those horrid monsters," she replied.

"You too?" Jakkon asked.

Tanyon ignored him and introduced everyone else.

"Do you happen to know the way back to the citadel?" Tari asked hopefully.

"Yes, in fact we are working our way there now," Kanea piped up. "You are welcome to join us."

Tari was overjoyed and tried to express her thanks.

Tanyon led the way with Kanea and Tari behind him and Jakkon behind them. The travel seemed peaceful, and no adventure seemed afoot at the moment. This peace pleased Kanea, whose thirst for adventure had been stretched to its limit. The princess had had enough adventure the past day to last her for weeks and would be very glad to return home. Tanyon felt similarly.

Tari and Jakkon, however, harbored different thoughts. Jakkon was puzzled by the beasts that had pursued them the previous day. *Why were they chasing us? What was that screeching noise? None of what happened makes much sense.* Tari's thoughts were different from Jakkon's. She wondered why the creature had chased her and not someone else. *Was it because Prince ran first? Or was there a deeper cause?* Like Jakkon, she could make sense of nothing.

The two girls made small talk, and Kanea realized that she had been one of the members of one team in the relay race.

"So, who were your partners?" the princess inquired.

"My older sisters," Tari replied. "We are referred to as the Helyanwe daughters or trio. The Dakiel triplets have been our rivals in the cross-country/relay race since we were five."

"Oh, how exciting! Have you won many?"

"This was our fourth win. The others have won four, and then others have been ties," the dukeling explained. On and on they talked. Jakkon listened but was rather bored.

Do all young ladies spend their rides discussing boring subjects? He yawned, but they were too busy laughing to hear.

Chapter Fourteen

Now *I am in a pretty situation.* Nic could not help thinking on his second day of captivity. He mentally beat himself as he thought of ways he could have prevented his capture. One full day plus some hours had now passed since he had last seen some familiar landmark. After Dibla and her henchmen had captured him, they had headed in a strange direction. From what he could guess, they were going to the princess' homeland, Crakaton.

The warriors, the dukeling, and the princess spent the night in the woods as they had before. During this time, conversation began to fill the void.

"What is the difference between fencing and sword fighting?" Tari asked.

Tanyon, who was examining his flat sword, looked up. Later he wondered if the question came because he had been fiddling with his weapon. Honestly, he was oblivious to the answer. Jakkon was resetting his crossbow but stopped to answer.

"Fencing is an art, while sword fighting is not," he replied, hoping that this answer would be satisfactory to the dukeling, but, alas, it was not.

"Could you be a tad more specific?"

"Fencing requires extreme skill and agility. Sword fighting requires a different kind of skill, and the same amount of agility, but it requires more strength. You see, a fencing sword is long and thin with a wrist guard."

"What is a wrist guard?" she interrupted.

"It is a curved sheet of metal that protects the wrist," Jakkon replied rather impatiently. "Now back to what I was saying. The kind of sword they use in what is called sword fighting is a flat blade that is wider and heavier than the fencing blade. The heavier swords are the usual choice for warriors."

"So, besides the choice of swords, there is no difference?" Kanea jumped into the conversation.

"No, there are other differences. Fencing requires lightness of foot, but with sword fighting one needs to stand his ground. Fencing is used for sport and for fun because there are rules—like any such game. Sword fighting techniques, on the other hand, was developed for war and battles," he finished, hoping not to have to explain any further. He was knowledgeable but not a teacher. Tari was satisfied completely, and Kanea was impressed with the information.

"My, Jakkon, yours was such a complete and understandable explanation. I never used to be able to decipher the difference, but what you said made it so clear." This compliment took him aback, and he did not know how to respond. Instead of speaking, he chose to merely bow and return to his crossbow.

Tanyon took the first shift and spent this time thinking. *Those beasts almost looked like wolves,* he thought, *but they were as big as horses, and those teeth…* He remembered the large, bear-like teeth that had flashed like knives. *Why were those beasts even in Pneutra? I have never seen or heard of anything like them.* Then his mind flashed back to his king. King Rigal had been hunting when he was attacked and slain by a creature. *Horrible beyond description* was how the one survivor had described the thing. *Interesting,* he thought.

Tanyon awakened Jakkon for the second watch, but he did not tell him his suspicions. Morning came much too soon for all of them. They mounted their horses and followed Tanyon, who was again relying on his lodestone. They started at a canter through the woods. Tari spied a fallen tree trunk and longed to jump it with Prince, but that was not their route. An hour must have passed when Tanyon said, "Let's stop."

"Why?" asked Jakkon, and he was rewarded with a look from the elder warrior.

"Riding for two days has worn on me," Tanyon replied. "Even a warrior like me needs a break."

The two girls agreed and allowed their horses to rest for a while. Tari's stomach growled, reminding her that she had not eaten for a day. Jakkon began scouring his saddle bags for something to satisfy himself.

"Aha!" he exclaimed and extracted some pieces of fruit. "I thought I had packed some." He passed them to his small party and bit into one himself. They were very grateful for some sort of nourishment.

"Good thinking, Kingerly," Tanyon complimented. "I think you have just saved us all."

Jakkon bowed extravagantly. "Jakkon Kingerly, at your service. Now shall we be off?"

"Indeed."

∾

Nic's Crakaton wolf stopped and growled. "What is it?" demanded the burly man in front of Nicoron. The wolf continued to growl. The man asked the princess what to do.

"Send out one of the large ones, Burladase," she replied from her scaly mount.

"Yes, your majesty," Burladase commanded a huge Crakaton wolf to scout the surrounding area. Nic wondered what could possibly be amiss.

∾

Tanyon untied the reins of his stubborn chestnut, which Jakkon had again left for him. As usual, the stallion stomped his hooves and bobbed his head.

"All right," Tanyon mumbled, "please be sweet for me again, will you." He lifted one foot into the left stirrup. Jakkon had already mounted his even-tempered mare and enjoyed watching his comrade-in-swords struggle with the glossy stallion. His attention was diverted to the bushes just beyond Tanyon.

"Did some—" he never finished his statement. One of the huge creatures that had chased them leaped out of the bushes. The chestnut spooked and ran. Tanyon landed flat on his back, completely vulnerable to the snapping jaws of the beast.

Kanea screamed and fainted into Tari's arms.

The beast saw the defenseless warrior and stalked toward Tanyon, placing a menacing paw on his broad chest.

"A little help, anyone!" Tanyon called out as the wolf-like monster lowered its dripping jaws over his head.

Whiz! Plunk! A bolt embedded itself in the monster's neck.

Tari, trying to awake the unconscious princess, turned to see Jakkon still holding his crossbow. They all stood there for a few moments, still taking in what had just happened.

Tanyon was the first to regain his composure. "Thank you, Jakkon, again," he said.

"No problem," Kingerly replied and returned his crossbow to its place on the horn of his saddle. Kanea regained her feet, and Tari mounted Prince.

"I wonder why that beast came after us," Tanyon thought aloud. He approached the dead creature.

"What are you doing, Tanyon?" Kanea inquired from her saddle.

"Somehow, I don't think these creatures are acting on their own," he thoughtfully replied.

"So are you looking for some sort of marking?" Tari asked.

"Yes." He did not need long to find that the creature was indeed branded, but the mark made no sense to him. The image was of a circle with a sword in the middle. Tanyon requested Jakkon to examine it. "What can you make of this, Kingerly?"

"It is hard to say," Jakkon replied. "The mark is uncommon, for sure, yet I seem to recognize it."

"Maybe it is the mark of a band," Tari suggested.

"I do not think so. Wait!" Jakkon snapped his fingers. "That is the ancient marking of Crakaton."

"Crakaton?!" the other three chorused.

"You must be jesting!" Kanea insisted.

"I am not. The Crakaton arms was a circle with a sword in the middle. The sword had blood dripping from it."

"But this marking doesn't have blood dripping from the sword," Tanyon countered.

"No, but it is the closest match I can think of. Besides, it would be difficult to imitate blood on a branding iron."

Tanyon and the others seemed to accept this possible explanation.

"Then do you think that King Trea San could be up to his old tricks again?" Tari approached a subject that the others seemed too afraid to approach.

"Impossible!" Tanyon objected vehemently. "Trea San lived over four hundred years ago. There is no possible way he could still be alive."

"Besides Crakaton lies in waste! It has no use," Kanea protested. "How could he possibly do anything with wasteland?"

"Actually, no one except Trea San and his people have ever been inside those treacherous mountains. So we have no real knowledge of the land," Jakkon clarified. "Not to mention the fact that Trea San and his people did not come from the same land we did." He paused for a moment. "In fact, we don't even know where we came from."

Tanyon came to a decision at last. "First and foremost, we need to return to the citadel, and then we can express our thoughts about Crakaton." The warrior reached into his pocket to retrieve his lodestone. "Oh, no!" he cried.

"What?" inquired the princess.

"When that creature placed his paw on my chest, he smashed my lodestone casing! It is useless now."

"How will we get back to the city now?" Tari was acutely concerned. First, she had been separated from her sisters by fierce creatures. Secondly, she had been lost, but then she had been found. Now they were all lost with no way of guiding themselves back to safety.

"I do not know," Tanyon replied, rather stricken by their state of affairs. "What I do know is that we can't just wait here. This attack proves that the beasts are still lurking about, and it would be better to keep moving."

"I could lead us by the stars," Jakkon suggested again.

"In the middle of the day?" Tanyon countered tersely.

"Well, what about using the position of the sun?" Tari pointed out.

"But it's noon," Kanea replied. "The sun is in the middle of the sky, so Jakkon couldn't tell us where we are."

"Goodness!" Tari murmured. "Now what?"

Tanyon thought for a moment. "For sure we cannot stay in this same place. If these wolf-monsters work like regular wolves, this one was a scout, meaning more are out there. If we stay here, the others will be able to hunt us with ease."

"So we definitely need to move," Jakkon agreed.

"Indeed, but *where* is the question," Tari stated.

"Anywhere but here," Tanyon finally decided. "We should be fairly safe if we stay together until nightfall. Then we will continue to camp and hope to find some village or hunters who will aid us."

Thus was their plan settled. Jakkon still thought they should travel during the night, but his word meant little with Tanyon leading.

The party of captors continued on. Nicoron found it interesting that these men did not ride horses, but the Crakaton wolves. Dibla did not ride a wolf, but her dragon. How she doted on the scaly, spindly creature! Whenever she and her warriors stopped, she would take off the saddle and massage the dragon's back. Dibla spoke softly to it and called it her "sweet one."

Nic thought the dragon looked despicable, but he found some things that were interesting about the beast. The ears, at first glance, seemed to be layers of folded skin with cartilage jutting through it, but when Screecher was searching for specific sounds, he could stretch the layers into a full circle that could move to catch certain sounds. Nevertheless, dragons had been an eternal symbol for plundering and death.

They finally stopped for a short break. Again, Nic was chained to a tree, which was not as comfortable as being on the furry hide of a Crak-wolf. Burladase looked around and made mention that the wolf they had sent out had not returned. He grunted. "That isn't good."

"What was that, Burladase?" Dibla asked, looking over the horny back of the Screecher. The dragon began moving its ears; obviously the creature had heard something in the forest.

"The Crakaton wolf that we sent out has not returned."

"That isn't good," Dibla repeated. "It must mean we're being followed."

Burladase began to bark orders. "Saddle up, double time! Get moving!" At these sharp words, everyone dropped what they had in their saddle bags and loaded the beasts with them. Nic was roughly slapped on the back of his ride and secured.

The wolf turned its head around to sniff him and growled. "What, you're now just realizing that I am on your back?" Nic mumbled to the animal. Someone jumped in front of him and kicked the thing in the ribs. It reared and began racing away with even, smooth strides.

"I will take to the air and meet you at the gate," Dibla announced before her dragon swept her into the skies. The pack of wolves and men bounded through the forest. The Crakaton wolves were amazingly rapid as they hastened on. Nic wondered how fast they were going, but eventually he stopped wondering, probably because he beginning to experience nausea.

The four continued at their canter. "I never thought I would get tired of riding," Tari mumbled, "but after this trek, Prince, I think I must give both of us a three-day break." Prince bobbed his head to the rhythm of his canter. Their private conversation was interrupted by Tanyon's exclamation. "I have found some tracks!"

They all reined in their horses, and the two warriors slipped from their steeds to examine their discovery.

"What kind do you think they are?" Kanea asked excitedly.

"It is hard to tell," Tanyon replied. "From the looks of it, a large party passed, so most of the tracks are disturbed."

"Think it could be a party going to Pneutra?" Tari inquired.

"It is possible," Jakkon agreed. "I say that we follow them."

"Sounds logical to me," Tanyon settled the matter, and they began following the promising tracks. The four were excited at the first sign of civilians they had for two days. So excited were they that they increased their speed to a gallop.

Prince's spirits had obviously risen because Tari noticed that he was taking the lead. She gently brought him behind Tanyon's chestnut. She began thinking about how elated her sisters would be when she returned. Then her thoughts trailed away to the terrible creatures that had chased them away from Pneutra's capital. From what they had found earlier that morning, the beasts carried the mark of Crakaton on them.

Crakaton had always had a name that brought fear to other cantons, but that had been years ago. Crakaton had been dormant for practically hundreds of years. Nothing had been heard or seen from it since the treacherous king had retreated into his fortress of a land. *Mystery? Adventure?* Tari wondered. *Riveting.*

Chapter Fifteen

BOTH PARTIES RODE throughout the day, not bothering
to stop for more than a few minutes. Night crept over
the horizon like a lizard over a stone. While Tanyon, Jakkon,
Kanea and Tari were resting, Nic was straining on the back of
an unruly beast. How Nicoron wished they would stop and
rest, but his captors pushed the wolves on. His journey would
not meet its end until the beginning of his fourth day.

It was dawn and Nic's rest had been nonexistent. His body
was weary and weak. For hours, he had nothing to sustain
him, and for days his food had not been nourishing enough.
This lack resulted in more than just weak body. Despair over-
took him, as he realized that four days and no rescue did not
mean anything promising. His mind was foggy, and he could
not think straight. Consequently, he despaired and wondered
if he had either been abandoned or forgotten. If his head had
been clearer, he would have been level enough to realize that
his family and his countrymen would not have forgotten him.

Suddenly the party skidded to a halt. The rider in front of
him dismounted from his wolf, and Nic saw, to his utter fear, a
rusty, iron gate. The gate itself was forty feet high and stretched
from mountain to mountain. Just like she had said, Dibla was

there to order the gate be opened. Crank and levers were heard groaning, and the lordling expected the huge gate to open, but what he expected didn't happen. In its stead, a smaller door about ten feet in height and width, opened in a corner. *So this is what the gateway to waste is like,* he thought.

Burladase, the chief of his kidnappers, came to him and dragged him off the beast.

"On your feet!" he demanded, but Nic was too weak to even stand on his own two feet. He fell to the ground without strength even to kneel. Burladase repeated his harsh order, "Stand! On your feet!"

Another captor shouted, "The boy is too weak. Put him on a wolf and let us go."

Burladase obeyed, knowing that he could not rely on the lordling to support his own weight. *Back on that stinking beast,* Nic groaned in despair, *and into the gates of wasteland.*

～

Tanyon awoke. His body was either not as sore as it had been, or his nerves were numbed from the rough conditions. His thoughts went to his days in the training academy when they had trained for rough conditions, but that was when he was thirteen.

"Too many years on a heather cot," he murmured to himself. Suddenly, he realized that he had woke up and had not been awakened. "Jakkon!" he shouted as he sat up.

"Yes?" replied the younger warrior.

"You did not wake me up!" Tanyon grumbled, trying not to appear foolish. Apparently, the others had allowed their weary leader to sleep in. Kanea and Tari were seated by a fire, roasting something.

"Is it not our fearless and ingenious leader?" Tari exclaimed. "Please, join us for some fresh deer."

"How did you obtain deer meat?" he inquired.

Tari explained that Princess Kanea had said she was tired of fruit, so she took Prince and hunted down a deer. "Jakkon did the skinning and gutting though. Me and Kanea roasted it."

"Kanea and I," corrected the princess, and Tari rolled her eyes. Tanyon jumped up from his place of rest.

"The meat is still hot," Jakkon cautioned. A few minutes passed as they all indulged in some rather unsavory meat. At the first bite, everyone had cringed at the taste, but the fare was better than what they had eaten for days.

"Does anyone want some seasoning?" Jakkon asked. Everyone looked up to see him holding a black glass vial.

"What would that be?" Tanyon asked.

"Seasoned salt."

"Is that redundant?" Tari inquired. "You know, salt is seasoning, so wouldn't seasoned salt be redundant?"

Jakkon gave her a wearied look. "I did not name it," he replied shortly. "Now would anyone like some for their venison?"

"I will take some," Kanea replied and received the vial and sprinkled some on her slice of meat. "How is it that you always seem to have everything we need?"

The supplier shrugged. "I prepare, I guess. I always think of the worst that would happen, and I prepare. Also, I like most of my meat with seasoned salt, which is usually not provided."

"Well, that's good," Tanyon said as he took the vial.

He then passed it to Tari. "Indeed," the dukeling added. "This seasoning makes the deer meat taste delicious."

Jakkon smiled and began eating his portion. His overbearing hunger devoured the remaining venison.

~

The party of men and gigantic wolves proceeded beyond the creaky gates. Nicoron sat upright on his wolf, finally realizing that he would be the first Pneutraite ever to see Crakaton on the inside. The lordling was in awe. The whole land was cut in a bowl shape, and Nic was on the "rim." In the heart of Crakaton were two steaming volcanoes right next to each other, and between them was a menacing fortress—the ancestral home of King Trea San.

"It is always good to see the Twins whenever we come home," Burladase sighed as he beheld the red sight.

Nic guessed that he was referring to the volcanoes. A beige color surrounded the mountains and covered most of the land, except for the far east. Gigantic trees of a horrible green color looked like a stain on cloth. Behind the volcanoes and surrounding the beige were the lavender mountain ranges creating the sides of the bowl.

Down they went. Nicoron expected the road to be steep, but somehow it wasn't. Crakatonians apparently were very advanced—at least advanced enough to smooth a road.

"This is nothing like a wasteland," Nic mumbled to himself so his captors could not hear. *Everyone has been wrong,* he thought. As they advanced, the lordling began to see the smaller picture. This landscape was the most unique of all. The beige was fields of grass, giant grass. He gasped as he beheld the six feet tall, three-inch in diameter grass that graced both sides of the lane. *And that was not even the largest!* He wondered how they could have built a straight road through the thickest bush on Levea. He turned his head left and right and saw nothing but the gigantic grass. Suddenly his wolf balked and growled at a blue, two-headed snake that had appeared.

"It has two heads!" he gasped.

Burladase chortled. "Indeed, it has two heads, and there's more beasts just as weird to you outsiders."

More? What does he mean? the boy wondered, but he didn't need to wonder long. His eyes wandered to the right side of the road, and he was astonished to see a small horse—a really small horse that could not have been two feet tall, but that wasn't what captured his attention. *What unusual coloring!* The body, neck, and legs were the same color as a chestnut, but the animal's mane and tail were pure white. Nic saw right beyond was another one exactly like it. The two miniature horses were startled by the commotion and ran away.

The ears of the wolf Nic rode perked up and turned left, then he heard a sharp shrill from that direction. He turned his head to see a green fox. *A green fox?* he mentally gasped. *What else does Crakaton have to offer?* The strangely colored animal had been heading toward the road but upon spotting the caravan, turned around.

He caught a glimpse of movement. His eyes shot upward to take in what he thought was a gigantic rabbit with antlers, but the sight was distorted. Part of him reasoned that the thing that he thought he saw could not have been, but the other part of him said that Crakaton could have anything behind its borders. Nic shook his head and refused to choose between the sides; he was just too tired to argue with himself.

∽

Four days of nigh onto constant riding had passed, and the four weary, lost youths were tired. The horses, except for Prince, were exhausted and refused to be ridden that day.

"Fitherlew, we cannot continue on our journey today. We should take off the day and rest," Jakkon advised.

"We cannot rest, Kingerly," Tanyon stood firm. "The sooner we return to the castle, the sooner we can take a much more luxurious time. Besides we do not have enough rations to sustains us for two days."

"But the horses refuse to allow us even near them with saddles in our hands," Jakkon protested.

"And what about the creature we encountered?" Tari piped up. "The sooner we get back to the capital of Pneutra, the sooner we can engage this dilemma."

"How can we get back to the citadel without horses? Ours will not let us ride them," Kanea joined.

Everyone lapsed into silence. *Ours is quite the dilemma to be in at this time.* Tanyon began to evaluate their situation and their choices. *We can take the day off, but we will lose precious time. We can keep going on foot, but that will be slower. That was something, or...* Tanyon suddenly smiled.

"I have a compromise!" he announced. All were eager to

hear this compromise, so he continued. "How about we rest half the day and then ride for the other half?"

"Brilliant!" squealed Kanea and Tari simultaneously.

Jakkon nodded. "Now I know why you were at the top of the strategy class."

"Yes, now you know why." Tanyon smiled. "So we all agree."

"Indeed," agreed Tari.

"I agree," Kanea stated, and the matter was settled.

∽

The unit of kidnappers and their captive continued riding through the forest of grass. *What an oxymoron,* Nic thought. *A forest of grass.* His worn body rested against the neck of the hairy wolf with his arms chained around it. The rest of the day was a blur. No excitement, no new creatures, nothing to keep Nicoron from falling into a restless slumber. They had entered this fortress-like country in the early morning, and when they reached the heart of it, the day had passed into evening afternoon.

Nic's heavy eyes slowly opened to see the astronomical, gray fortress wedged between the two billowing volcanoes. It seemed to him that most things in this country were of interesting magnitudes. Finally, after four days of nearly constant riding, he was taken from the back of the Crak-wolf and was forced to walk on his anemic legs. This time he had no pitying captor to save him. He stumbled several times before reaching the passageway into the courtyard of the fortress.

The Crakaton courtyard was the most gray and dull one that Nic had ever seen. *Tedious would probably be a better adjective,* he thought to himself. He was used to seeing foliage; Crakaton had only stone and war-training equipment. This sight alarmed him. *War-training equipment is only used for training for war—not for anything else. Why would there be training equipment in a courtyard?* he thought, but nothing good came to mind.

Dibla strolled down some side stairs. He grimaced at her apparently sweet smile. "I see you have transported our *invitee* safely." She laced her words with a sugary tone. "How pleased my father will be."

"Invitee? More like prisoner," Nicoron retorted.

"Oh, do not be so bad-tempered, Nic," she snapped. "After all, this little escapade is just beginning, and we do not want you to ruin it yet." She turned to her henchmen. "Now, lead our *guest* to his quarters."

Burladase laughed once and pushed his prisoner in the direction of an iron door underneath the stone stairs that Dibla had descended. One man opened the door while Burladase pushed him into the obsidian darkness.

"Someone, grab a torch!" Burladase ordered, and one of his captors produced a torch. He then lit something on the both sides of the wall, and the entire corridor seemed to come alive with light. Though he was relieved by the light, what he saw was not encouraging—rows of cells, prison cells. *Oh right, not a prisoner,* he thought sarcastically.

The Crakatonian guards threw him into the first prison cell they came to. The door clanked shut, leaving Nic to wonder if he would ever see the outside of the door.

~

Half the day was spent on recuperation, and the four were grateful for the rest when the time for riding came. Jakkon mounted his black mare and patted her affectionately.

"I think I am getting really attached to this horse," he said. "Can we name them?"

Tanyon looked back at him from his chestnut horse. "I think they have numbers instead of names."

"I know that, but can we name them?"

"Name yours. We shall see if anyone back home cares. Now let's get in some galloping."

Jakkon decided to name his mare Midnight Star after the white star that was on her forehead.

Tanyon began thinking about naming his chestnut. "What would you like to be called, friend?" Tanyon asked the horse. "You have been very good lately."

The chestnut threw back his head, neighed, and all the horses increased their speed from a canter to full gallop, inspiring a name.

"How is Desert King? *Desert* for your color and *King* for your leadership qualities."

The chestnut neighed again. From that time on, Desert King (informally known as King) was labeled as Tanyon's mount, and Midnight Star (Midnight) was labeled as Jakkon's horse by all the warriors.

On they rode. Afternoon turned into evening, and evening turned into night. The riders still persisted.

"Fitherlew!" called Jakkon from the back, and he reined in

Desert King.

"What is it, Kingerly?"

"I do not like these tracks."

"What is it about them that you don't like?" Kanea asked, annoyed that they had stopped.

"Well, could horses create such destruction? Look at these branches." Kingerly slid off Midnight and showed them a bush, whose branches had been broken by something violent.

"If these horses or people were running fast enough and in great number, yes, they could have caused such destruction to the shrub," Tari replied. "Anything else?"

"My spirit does not have peace about this trail," he responded in an irritated voice.

"Honestly?" Kanea piped up.

"Yes, honestly." He sighed. "It's just that I like to trust my intuition, and it doesn't seem rather peaceful right now."

Tanyon Fitherlew looked back. "According to our agreement, I am leader. And I say we go this way," he added stubbornly.

The others did not resist but obediently mounted their horses and followed Tanyon. Jakkon's mind would not allow him to simply settle; he knew something was amiss even if Tanyon did not.

Chapter Sixteen

I n their exhaustion, the four travelers had slept away the evening and part of the morning. Once they had awakened, Jakkon and Tanyon set about trapping a few rabbits for their breakfast, which had taken a while. It wasn't until noon before they resumed riding. Is it not getting warmer?" asked Tari as she mounted her horse with the others.

"Must be a south wind from Dakiel coming through," Jakkon replied.

"All the way into Pneutra?" Kanea spoke with a concern.

Jakkon stopped.

"Why are we stopping, Kingerly?" the front man inquired.

"It is getting warmer, is it not?"

"Yes," they all replied.

"It is fall, and we are warm—probably with a south Dakielite wind," Jakkon stated.

"Indeed," Tanyon answered. "Is there a problem?"

"Yes, a south Dakielite wind, a strong one at that." Tanyon turned his horse to face everyone else, but none of them seemed to catch what Jak was thinking.

"Strong Dakielite winds do not reach Pneutra very often—especially during the autumn."

When he had finished, Tari began to comprehend what he had been intimating. "In other words, we have been going south or west, instead of north!"

"Oh, no!" Tanyon exclaimed. "So we're lost!" The other three looked at him.

"Catch up, fearless leader," Jakkon mumbled.

Tari threw her head back and laughed, but suddenly stopped. "Mountains peaks," she murmured.

"What was that, Tari?" Kanea asked.

"Mountains peaks—I think I can see mountains peaks."

Tanyon perked up. "Mountains peaks could mean we're close to Langhen," Tanyon offered.

"Langhen does get strong south winds, but Crakaton would," Jakkon added somberly. "And Crakaton has the most pronounced mountain range in Levea."

They all became silent. Tanyon made the first move. He encouraged Desert King toward the only hope they had had.

"Tanyon, what are you doing?" Jakkon stopped their leader. "Crakaton has never had a very hospitable history."

"We don't even know if Crakaton lies in that direction."

"No, but there is a fifty percent chance that it does," Jakkon countered.

Tanyon sighed. "Indeed, but maybe we can find some hunters or such nearby."

"Why would hunters be near here?" Tari asked.

"I do not know why, but I do know that hunters have been around Crakaton's borders…that is if we are seeing Crakaton's ranges." Tanyon was about to explain further when Kanea interrupted. "Oh, so you're thinking that we could possibly find Pneutraite hunters, and they could lead us home!"

"Indeed." Tanyon responded simply. "Now let's go."

Jakkon was again uneasy about this decision but took his place at the rear. The horses sensed the change in mood and lifted their hooves more eagerly. Any onlooker would only guess that they missed their stalls and oats. The peaks came closer every minute. They rode for what seemed only a few short minutes before they came to a clearing of trees surrounded by bushes. Tanyon motioned for them to stopped, and he dismounted from King.

"Everyone, dismount. Tari, you and the princess can guard our horses while Jakkon and I scout ahead," he ordered.

"Scout? Do you think there could be danger?" Kanea was instantly alarmed.

"Precautions are mandatory when you are in a place you do not know."

"You *never* said that before on this escapade," Kanea retorted, somewhat annoyed.

The warrior replied, "If I kept that rule, we would be moving about as slow as a snail."

Before anything else could be said, he dragged Jakkon through the bushes. Kanea was rather puzzled by all this subterfuge. Tanyon and Jakkon had discovered that the woods were thinning rather rapidly. The elder had seen this coming and wanted to give the ladies enough coverage in case anything happened. From what he could see through the trees, they were nearing the base of the mountains.

"Tanyon, look!" Jakkon pointed ahead at the rusty gate at the base of the mountain.

"So people do live in Crakaton!" he muttered.

"Indeed, and I am guessing that they wouldn't like us poking our noses around here," Jakkon noted.

"Let's just get a closer look," Tanyon replied.

"When have you ever been the adventurous one?" Jakkon retorted as he followed his fellow soldier, who was already advancing. They swiftly slid behind trees for concealment. Soon both were at the edge of the tree line, and Tanyon motioned for them to stop there. Jakkon stared at the colossal passageway into the unknown land.

"That fort is huge!" He whispered to Tanyon. The other nodded in acknowledgment but did not speak. Jakkon's eyes wandered up the base of the mountains. The seemingly black elevations never ended its ascent, and the cross-bow wielder could not see the summits of these steep fault-block mountains. While Kingerly was admiring the scenery, Tanyon Fitherlew was observing the guards at the gate. Their attire was black leather, something other cantons did not use, and they were heavily armed. He saw that they were cocky and rather inattentive to their border; but most of all, he saw that they were celebrating. Tanyon's interest was piqued.

"Jakkon."

"Yes, Fitherlew."

"Might you have a gazing tube?"

"You mean a miniature telescope?"

"Whatever it is called."

"Here it is," Jakkon handed his fellow a silver tube. "Wait, how did you know I had a miniature telescope?"

"Because you have always had the most useful items on this extemporaneous journey," Tanyon responded with a smile as he received the tool. He lifted it to his right eye and examined the Crakatonian guards.

"What do you see?" Jakkon inquired eagerly.

"The guards are celebrating, it seems, and they are drinking something out of a green bottle. They laugh and slap each other on the back." Tanyon stopped and asked if Jakkon would have another lens to enlarge the image. The lens was passed.

"They are speaking."

"Hand the scope to me. I can read lips," Jakkon stated.

"Can you?" Tanyon was surprised yet again.

"Yes, now do you want me to tell you what they are saying or not?" He grinned as he received his instrument and spied through it.

"What are they saying?"

"The guards are moving too much for me to make out anything," he said at first. "Uh-oh, another guard just walked into view. He seems to be a higher-ranking officer. He ordered one of the guards to put away the drink. They complain and resist, so he took the bottle and threw it on the ground."

"This officer doesn't sound very calm," Tanyon noted.

"Not at all, my friend," Jakkon replied. "He says that their princess wants them to be vigilant—not drunk. What do you suppose that means?"

"So Crakaton has a princess."

"Indeed. Oh, one of the guards asks why they always get orders from the princess and not Trea San himself."

"What did the officer say?"

"To do it or else—well, just or else," Jakkon informed. "The lesser guards seem to accept that and are—uh-oh. Hide!" Both ducked behind the trees.

"We should return to Princess Kanea and Dukeling Tari," Tanyon decided.

"Now that is the Tanyon Fitherlew I know," the younger joked, and they turned to go, but something caught their attention. "Wait Tanyon!"

"Now what?"

"Look," Jakkon pointed to his far left. Out of the bushes emerged the same kind of monsters that had been chasing them before, only this time with leather-clad men riding them.

"Crakaton has been training those monsters!" Tanyon breathed.

Jakkon raised his telescope to his eye. "Interesting." Jakkon mused. "They train the wolves so that they can ride them. Oh, they are talking again!" He adverted his attention back to the turrets in the gate.

"The wolves?" Tanyon snapped his head back.

"No, the men!" Jakkon sneered. "Uh-oh."

"What now?"

"Tanyon, look at this," Jakkon handed his friend the spyglass. "Look at what the man has in his hand."

"It is a sword."

"The other man then," Jakkon clarified.

"He has a cloak," Tanyon responded.

"Look at that cloak carefully," the younger instructed.

"It looks familiar, but I do not know from where…" Suddenly, Tanyon gasped. "That cloak belonged to one of our lordlings."

"Exactly!" Jakkon snatched the spyglass. "And how would a Crakatonian soldiers encounter a lordling's cloak?"

"If they kidnapped him…" Both warriors were now thinking along the same lines.

"This seems a bit too coincidental—especially since that fierce overseer just mentioned Lordling Nic's full name," Jakkon added grimly.

"So what you're saying is that Crakatonian soldiers kidnapped Lordling Nicoron Salindone and attacked us with those trained wolf monsters and probably that dragon too," Tanyon clarified.

"Exactly."

"We need to get back to the princess and Tari." Tanyon was now ready to go.

⁓

As Tari and Kanea waited nervously for their protectors' safe return, an awkward silence fell between them.

"Have Tanyon and Jakkon always been your personal guards?" Tari finally asked.

"No," Kanea replied in a somewhat gloomy tone. "Nicoron Salindone and Denel Quariopel were my guards. They are two young, brave lordlings of excellent families."

"Then why are we stuck with Sword and Stars?" The dukeling asked. Kanea chuckled.

"Well, Nic and Denel needed to participate in the Nobling Duels. They teamed up for sword fighting, you know."

"Oh…" Suddenly, something clicked in Tari's brain. "Wasn't Nicoron the lordling who disappeared on Horsey Day?"

"Yes. Yes, he was," Kanea answered.

"I tied with his younger brother Asher in the jumping competition."

"Oh, I remember that!" The princess brightened up. "You two were fabulous! Was it a difficult competition?"

"Asher is an impressive rider. He kept Prince and I hopping, literally." Both laughed at the play on words.

"So did you just meet Asher?" Kanea inquired with a hint in her voice Tari knew well from her sisters.

"I have seen him before, but we never got to meet each other formally until this year." Tari changed the subject to something other than Asher and herself. They continued to talk about the games, and then they moved onto horses and other such subject that girls enjoy conversing about.

After what seemed like hours, their two young warriors burst through into the clearing.

"What is there to report?" The princess asked.

"We are about a half mile from the very gate into Crakaton's barren landscape," Jakkon announced with a dramatic flair.

Tari gulped. "That's not good, is it?"

"No, not at all," Princess Kanea responded.

"There is something else," Tanyon added.

"What?" the princess prodded.

"The Lordling Nicoron Salindone is now the prisoner of

the most unfriendly canton in Levean history," Jakkon blurted out without thinking.

Kanea stood stricken by the news.

"Jakkon, you might need to explain that a little more," Tanyon whispered in Jakkon's ear.

"When we were spying at the Crakatonian gate, we saw warriors talking about Lordling Nicoron and holding his cloak."

"Please, you are not telling me that my personal guard is in the clutches of the Crakaton?"

"I am telling you exactly that," Jakkon replied.

Kanea was now staring into space. Then she fainted. Tari's agile body slipped off Prince and caught the princess before she slipped to the ground. Well, she actually padded Kanea's fall as opposed to stopping it.

"Gentlemen, I think the past few days have been a bit too much for her highness," Tari concluded.

"You're telling me," Jakkon muttered, wondering how so much could happen in a few seconds.

Tanyon fetched a little water and sprinkled it on the princess' face. She regained consciousness and asked, "What are we going to do about this situation?" Once she had gained a full sense of what had just been brought to their attention, Tari helped her to her feet.

"We were hoping you could decide that for us," Jakkon responded.

Kanea stared off into space yet again.

"Please don't faint again, your highness," Tari pleaded.

This time the princess did not faint; instead she mounted

her horse. "I think it would be wise to return to the citadel and bring reinforcements."

With that decision, everyone mounted in preparation to leave. Tanyon took the lead and pushed Desert King into a trot. Suddenly, the horse balked.

"What now?" Tanyon was exasperated by the horse's behavior, but when he looked up, he could see why the horses were balking. Something loomed over him that was at least ten feet tall with antlers that formed the most beautiful rack he had ever seen.

"A…a…jackrabbit?" Jakkon whispered at the loudest decibel he could muster. The jackrabbit merely stared at them.

Kanea nearly fainted; Tari's mouth was wide open.

Tanyon tried to speak, but his voice had fled.

The jackrabbit continued to stare them down with piercing black eyes. They became aware of a padding sound around them. More jackrabbits—six to be exact—appeared and surrounded them. The first opened his mouth. "I, Antlre, with the power invested in me as king of jackrabbits, do hereby take ye humans into my custody as prisoners."

The four now prisoners were astounded. *They can speak.* Jakkon thought. *And we are their prisoners. Great!*

Tanyon finally found his voice and began to speak, but the gigantic rabbit shushed him. "Close thy mouth, Crakatonian warrior. Ye shall be able to present thy case before the Council of Jackrabbits. Until then ye four have the right to be silent. Now dismount."

They obediently dismounted. Desert King began to rear,

but one shriek from a jackrabbit suppressed his rebellion. Antlre ordered them to discard their weapons. At first the warriors were resistant to this command, but the princess ordered them to comply. Kanea was prudent enough to see that if the foursome did not acquiesce to their captors' order, there could be some bloodshed.

"Now march!" Antlre demanded, and they began walking behind the king. Tari frowned as the jackrabbits led them through the creepy woods. Several times Jakkon thought of attacking the jackrabbit that held their weapons, but each time he considered the sharp antlers that each of their captors possessed. It would be foolhardy to try, and his attempt would surely end in failure. They were not forced to walk long before they emerged from the forest. Tanyon saw the base of the Crakaton/Pneutra border.

"Where are you taking us?"

"Interesting that ye did not ask sooner," Antlre commented. "We are taking thee to the Council of Jackrabbit to pay for ye crimes."

"What crimes?" Kanea blurted.

"Did ye not slay seven of our kind last week?"

"Of course not."

"That is exactly what the culprit would say," Antlre snapped. He began sniffing around a large rock, finally tapping three times in a rhythmic manner on the rock, which suddenly moved on its own. The prisoners were forced to march closer.

Tanyon, who was first in line, saw that the stone was actually the door to a tunnel that sloped down underneath the base of the mountains. The captives continued forward under the uncomfortable watch of the jackrabbits.

Tari's mouth dropped wide in despair when the rock door fell shut behind them.

The tunnel was nothing like one would imagine, and there was a greenish glow throughout the corridor. All were in awe of their surroundings, except the jackrabbits who kept them moving.

Tanyon observed that the walls of the tunnels were adorned with seashells and rocks like the halls of the citadel in Pneutra. *Interesting,* he thought. Suddenly they came out of the passageway into a large cathedral-like room. Apparently, many tunnels led here. Tanyon took note of the stone ledge in the far corner of the room. Below the high ledge was a circle outlined in seashells. Two of the jackrabbits led away their horses.

"Where are you taking them?" Jakkon shouted, but he was forced back by the piercing antlers of the giant rabbits.

"Welcome to the Council of Jackrabbits," Antlre announced, and the four were pushed into the center of the circle. Thumping noises came from other corridors, and more jackrabbits appeared.

"These new jackrabbits don't have antlers." Jakkon whispered to Tanyon who nodded in reply. Antlre and his companions hopped onto the ledge while the newcomers surrounded the four.

"What have the Sons of the Kings found this time?" asked one of the antlerless jackrabbits.

"The possible slayers of our fellow jackrabbits," Antlre responded. "They have been brought before thee to be judged by thee, Elder."

"We have nothing to do with the slaying of those seven jackrabbits," Jakkon protested.

"Silence, human," Elder snapped. "Thou shalt be tried and judged properly."

For the jackrabbits to situate themselves to their comfort took a few minutes, but once that was over, the real trial began.

Jakkon did not enjoy the way that the elders looked at him.

"Ye there," The elder flicked his ear in Tanyon's direction, and the warrior stepped forward. "Where were ye two weeks past at even time?"

"Training—"

"Aha! Training, dost thou elders see that this warrior is the slayer of our dear brethren?"

"But, Elder," objected Antlre. "Ye did not allow the boy to finish what he started to say."

He turned to Tanyon. "Training for what?"

"Training my trainees-of-war."

"Art thou preparing for war?"

"Not that I know of," Tanyon replied.

"Then why would ye be training your young ones to fight?" Antlre asked.

"To fail to prepare is to prepare to fail," he quoted a famous phrase.

Antlre cocked his head at the warrior's reply, and then his ear twitched. A young rabbit hopped close to Tanyon and began sniffing him.

"Ye may step down," Antlre said once the jackrabbit had finished sniffing him. Each of the four went through a similar interrogation. Tanyon and Jakkon bristled when the young jackrabbit hoped next to Kanea and began sniffing her. Suddenly, the beast jumped back and screeched.

"King Antlre!" the king of jackrabbits leaped from the stone ledge and looked where the younger was pointing with his ear.

"What is it?" Kanea asked a tad worried.

"It is the other half!" Antlre gasped.

"The other half of what?" Tari blurted.

"The other half of the Rigalian medallion!" Antlre exclaimed then he bowed before the princess; the other jackrabbits followed suit. "We are at thy command."

The four prisoners were immediately taken aback.

"I—I do not understand," the princess said.

"Ye do not know how much that decoration ye hath is worth?" Antlre queried. "Council of Jackrabbits, I have just cleared these four humans of any suspicion; they are now our honored guests."

Tanyon stepped back. "This is a bit much for my brain."

"Me too," Jakkon agreed.

Antlre called the Sons of the King and gestured to them. "These are my brethren and sons, princes of our kind; I am King Antlre of the jackrabbits."

"Please tell me why this medallion of mine is so important to you," Kanea demanded.

Antlre began to relate his story. "Years ago, when jackrabbits roamed the whole of Levea and not just Crakaton, Rigalian, king of Pneutra, promised my ancestors that the Pneutraites would never hunt jackrabbits. To seal this promise, he broke his medallion in half, giving half to us and keeping the other. He said that he would pass his half to his descendants as to keep this commitment sealed forever."

"I remember something like that in history," Kanea commented. "But I always thought of it as being a myth."

"Oh, it is anything but that," Antlre declared as another jackrabbit deprived of antlers approached, carrying a leaf very carefully. Jakkon marveled at how Antlre's paws could pick up the object much like a human's hands. "This is the half given to us by Rigalian."

Kanea placed her medallion next to Antlre's, and the two fit together perfectly.

"Incredible!" Jakkon muttered.

"My father told me that this was truly special, but…" Kanea's voice faltered, "I never thought it would have been like this…"

While the four were marveling at the united Rigalian medallion, a small jackrabbit hopped up to Antlre and whispered something in his ear. Antlre nodded and then turned to the four. "I do have some tidings that might be of some importance to you," he began.

"Please continue," Kanea prodded.

"Yesterday a prisoner was brought into Crakaton, and if my scouts are correct, then he is of thy canton."

"Do you know his name?" Tanyon inquired with an excited tone.

"Nik-run Salad-dome or something of the sort," Antlre replied, and Jakkon chuckled. Tanyon shot him stern stare.

"King Antlre, do you know why the Crakatonians would want Nicoron Salindone?" Tanyon asked, stressing the correct pronunciation of the lordling's name.

"There are few reasons the Crakatonians would desire to capture another nobling. During the war centuries ago, they kidnapped many of thine to torture for information."

"Do you think that they kidnapped Nic to torture him?" Kanea gasped.

"Aye, that would be the only way," Antlre nodded.

Kanea turned to the others. "We have to save him!" she cried.

Tanyon and Jakkon looked at each other. "Your highness," Tanyon replied, "we are hardly of the means to save him now. Perhaps if we found our way back to the citadel and then came back with an army. Right now, we are two young warriors, an overly excited dukeling, and you, princess."

Tari frowned. "Overly excited?" she murmured, but her terse comment was ignored.

Kanea spoke up again. "What if that takes too much time? What if by the time you get back, it is too late?"

Tanyon opened his mouth to speak, but she continued, "If King Antlre is correct and the Crakatonians do have him to torture him for information, then we have no time to wait!"

"True," Tari agreed. "If the Crakatonians kidnapped Nic for information, then that probably means they are planning another attack. If Nic keeps his mouth shut, we should be fine to take our time, but if he does not, then we need to act fast before this King Trea San tries to take over the world again."

Tanyon groaned.

Tari looked around. "What?"

"You are not helping me," Tanyon muttered.

"Indeed, Dukeling Tari," Jakkon replied. "We are supposed to keep the princess safe—not abandon our post for a nobling."

Despite the warriors' efforts, Kanea was undeterred. "I will not abandon Nicoron to torture and death!" she decided. "Now here is what will we do with the help of the jackrabbits. Tanyon and Jakkon will infiltrate the Crakaton fortress, find wherever Nic is, and bring him back here. Then we will go back to the citadel and tell the other royalty about the rise of Crakaton."

Tanyon and Jakkon sighed; they could not deny the princess' order.

"Very well, Princess Kanea," Tanyon agreed reluctantly. "But if that be, I need to be the one in charge."

Kanea gave him the authority. Tanyon turned to Antlre. "King Antlre, we need your help rescuing Nicoron Salindone."

As the jackrabbit king bowed at his request, Tari dodged his pronged antlers.

"We are at your disposal. Now just follow me," he added.

With Antlre as their guide, the foursome were given a full tour of the jackrabbit tunnels which took several hours, no matter how much Tanyon tried to divert their attention to the poor nobling in the dungeons of the Crakatonian fortress.

Jakkon, on the other hand, had a lot of questions. "What is this glowing substance?" the crossbow wielder asked.

"This is a glowing algae that groweth in the swamp here. We harvesteth it as a light source and a delicious snack; it is also a great fertilizer for our crops."

"Your kind has crops?" Tanyon exclaimed.

"The soil in Crakaton may be fertile, but it does not grow carrots large enough to satisfy our stomachs," Antlre explained. Suddenly, a little green creature darted past them.

"What was that?" Tari gasped.

"That is a fox," Antlre said.

"A glowing *green* fox?" Tari found it hard to believe, especially when a female jackrabbit came running after it.

"Greeny, come back to mama!" the female called to it.

"The glowing algae grows on their fur. Jackrabbits wrangle the foxes, and then harvest the algae from them," Antlre further explained.

"Another question…" Jakkon continued. "Why do only a few have antlers?"

"Why this is I do not know, but throughout our history only the royal males have ever had antlers. I am the eldest of my 265 siblings; therefore, I am king and have antlers. My sons and brethren, we call the Sons of the King, as is tradition. They are the ones who accompanied me when I captured thee." The tour continued throughout the tunnels.

"What are the monsters that the soldiers ride?" Jakkon inquired.

"They are called Crakaton wolves or Crak-wolves." Antlre replied.

"Do they bother your kind?" Tari piped up.

"Not much, but often my scouts have had to run for their lives. Crak-wolves loveth a chase, particularly with us," Antlre responded.

Tanyon decided that he should ask a question. "What are the Crakatonian defenses like?"

"King Trea San hath a single fortress in the heart of Crakaton wedged in between the Twin volcanoes—a precarious land. He liveth like a hermit, and no one has seen him since his coronation day."

"Does he keep a dungeon there?" Tanyon inquired.

"Yes, and it is the only one in Crakaton that I know of. The village has a jail, but any prisoners are rapidly transferred to the dungeon."

"King Antlre, do you have an exit near the Crakatonian dungeon?"

"Not directly near it," Antlre confessed. "In fact, our nearest one is five miles away. Ye see, the Crakatonian people have hunted us for centuries, so ye may be able to understand our wariness of them. We try to bring the slayers to justice, but very few of my subjects are plucky enough to capture them." He shook his head with chagrin.

Tanyon's mind was strictly focused on saving Nicoron Salindone. "We will need you to take us to your outlet nearest the dungeon, and then we are going to need some sort of guide," the warrior told King Antlre.

"Should we have a plan, Tanyon?" Jakkon pointed out.

"I have a plan, Jak, but it will only get us in sight of the fortification. From then on, we will have to wing it."

"When have I ever known you to 'wing' it?" Jakkon raised a brow and smiled, and his fellow gave him a flat look.

"You cannot build a scheme when you do not know even the terrain you will be encountering," Tanyon retorted.

"Just explain the plan," Tari moaned.

"All right, here is the plot: Jakkon and I exit through the exit nearest the fortress. We will find a lookout to spy on the fort. Once there, we will formulate a new plan based on the terrain." He looked at the ladies. "You two will stay here in the jackrabbit tunnels and be safe."

"Understood," Kanea replied meekly.

"So Antlre, please lead the way to the nearest exit," Jakkon declared with a wave of his fist. "We are going to save a lordling." The excited crossbow wielder let out a war cry.

"Good luck," Tari muttered. "And we shall stay here, bored."

Antlre bounded through the tunnels with Tanyon and Jakkon following. Many declarations of "Make way for the King" were heard as they raced about the catacombs. Finally, Antlre skidded to a stop and kicked at the ceiling. Light poured into the burrow as a covered door flew open. Antlre offered his height as a way for them to leave the catacombs and then nimbly jumped out of the hole and closed the door.

"Amazing!" Tanyon awed at their surroundings. Apparently, the opening nearest the fort was in a swamp. All around were gigantic trees covered in a green, drippy moss. Tanyon and Jakkon made their way through the precarious slough, trying not to step in the capricious puddles of muddy brown water covered in such a thick layer of algae and muck that it seemed like solid ground. Several times Jakkon nearly landed in one of those filthy pools. Antlre offered himself as their guide and their possible escape buggy. Once out of the nasty greenness, Antlre suggested they ride on his back.

"Are you sure?" Jakkon questioned.

"Anything for the servants of the Princess Kanea," Antlre replied as they mounted. They soon found out that it would be quite a bumpy ride. Nevertheless, riding was faster than traveling on foot. The swiftness of the animal was amazing to both young men.

"I didn't know that an animal could be this fast," Jakkon shouted to Tanyon.

"And I thought you knew everything," Tanyon teased.

That was the extent of their conversation of that trip for the wind whipping around them made it hard for anyone to talk or hear. Much faster than any person could have imagined, Antlre announced that they had arrived. "If ye head west over that ridge, then ye will see the fortress below," Antlre instructed. "I dare not go any closer."

Tanyon thanked their friend profusely, and Antlre insisted that he had only performed his duty. Then he disappeared into the evening mist.

Nicoron slept from morning until evening when Burladase awakened him. "It is time for your interrogation," the captain of Crakaton grinned maliciously as he dragged the chained boy from the cell. He pushed Nic out of the dungeons and prodded him mercilessly into the courtyard. Men wearing black leather trappings were training with more vigor than the lordling had ever seen. Nic stopped for a moment to watch the grueling workout.

"You, Number 67!" The trainer cracked his whip at a wearied soldier. "No slack!" Then the trainer whipped the slacker.

Burladase pushed Nic onward. A warrior opened a door on the other side of the courtyard/training facility. He saw the staircase on the other side of the door before Burladase shoved Nicoron up the steps. At the top of the stairs, he saw a hallway with seven doors—three on the left, three on the right, and one straightforward. One door on the left was ajar, and Nic was roughly guided to that door.

"Welcome to the interrogation center. This is where all naughty customers are brought," Burladase cackled and forced Nic into a chair, the only furniture in the cube.

⌒

Jakkon admired the composition of most of the land, awed by elephantine grasses and the musty air they produced. The dark evening produced an even eerier effect. The volcanoes towered over everything in the land; an orange hue hung around the tops of the steamy mountains.

"Everything here is so strange," he mused.

"Jakkon, get focused! We can explore this land after we retrieve Lordling Nicoron and do anything else that might need to be done," Tanyon reproached him. "Now let's creep up the hill and take a closer look at their defenses so we can form a plan of action."

With all the stealth the two warriors could muster, Tanyon

and Jakkon ascended the ridge and laid down on the smelly soil. The Twin volcanoes were black with soot and age and wedged between them was the imposing fort. A massive tower had been built into the volcano itself; the imposing garrison was too large to fit between the two steaming mountains alone, and it hung before them like an aged man's belly over his belt.

"Jakkon, the spyglass."

"Here," Jakkon extracted the piece of equipment from his tunic and handed the device to his friend. After some careful observation on Tanyon's part, the elder formed a plan.

"We will move south, then west and sneak around the east side of the fortress and to the gate, steering clear of the mountains. The soldiers in the turrets will not spot us directly below them. We take out the guards at the gate and switch clothes. Then we can easily find Nic and take him out of there. The cover of darkness will be very advantageous."

"You make it seem so simple," Jakkon shook his head wistfully. "If only it would be so…"

Tanyon turned to look at him. "Are you second guessing this mission?"

"I only wish it were as easy as you explained it."

"We must do this, Jak—no matter what. Our duty as warriors is to protect the nobility and royalty of our canton. That is why we have been trained," Tanyon placed a firm hand on Jakkon's shoulder. "Are you with me?"

Jakkon returned the gesture. "To the end!"

"Do not say that!"

"It always sounds so commendable in the stories."

"That is because we all know that the tales end well. We do not know how this will end." With the end of the conversation, they crept along the ridge, trying not to attract any attention. Tanyon guessed that the guards would be nonchalant about guarding because they had nothing against which to guard except wild animals, and his guess was correct. Once on the blind side of the turrets, the duo dashed down the steep incline and made a beeline for the wall. Tanyon could feel the cold stones through his clothing and leather armor as he flattened himself against the wall, and the frostiness of the wall sent uncomfortable chills throughout his body. He glanced back to ensure that Jakkon was still behind him before inching his way along the vast barrier. A few minutes passed that seemed like hours.

"Tanyon—" Jakkon cried, but his call was cut short.

"What is it, Jak—Jakkon?" When Tanyon did not hear a reply from his friend, he turned around to see that Jakkon was no longer behind him. Then he noticed an opening in the stones that had not been there when he passed; he approached slowly.

"Jakkon!" Tanyon whispered fiercely into the darkness. When he heard nothing, he decided to move forward into the inkiness. The warrior saw a glint on the ground and picked it up. *A flint and steel ignitor!* Squeezing the handle, a small yellow flame glowed in the gloom, reminding him of the three-day vigil after King Rigal's death and seeing the candles and torches lit in each window throughout Pneutra's citadel. He repeated Jakkon's name as he pressed forward.

"Here!" came an anemic reply.

"Jakkon, is that you?" Tanyon's hopes were heightened.

"Yes," Jakkon replied as he got up and dusted himself off. "I think I unwittingly pressed a stone that opened this cavern. And that is mine." He took the flint and steel from Tanyon.

"Well, let us just escape this inkwell and get back on track," Tanyon admonished then a scraping sound caused them to look back to the entrance. The two watched with horror as their only way out slammed shut.

"No, not now!" Tanyon cried as he rushed to the wall and tried to force the door open. After futile efforts of trying to pry their way out, Tanyon leaned against the wall and sank to the floor. The ignitor had since gone out.

"I have failed miserably," Tanyon mumbled.

"We have both failed miserably," Jakkon corrected as he too sank down next to his companion. Both sat in their misery and despair, but Jakkon found some heart left in him. "But we cannot fail! We must do this, Tanyon, remember? Pneutra may depend on it; Levea may depend on it! Come now, let us 'quit like men' as the ancient parchments would say."

"What does that even mean?" Tanyon grumbled, still wallowing in his despair.

"How do men quit?" Jakkon asked him, and when Tanyon was not able to answer, he answered his own question. "They do not! Men do not quit. We do to the death. So come, friend; let's do this until the end."

They rose together, and Jakkon lit the ignitor.

"Look!" Jakkon pointed to the far corner. "Is that a staircase?"

They investigated and were relieved to see that there were stairs, possibly their way out. The two warriors ascended the windy steps. Jakkon had lit the ignitor four times when the stairs faded away to a level hallway, and at the end of the hall was a door. Jak felt like cheering, but that could've alerted any occupants of the castle who were near. Tanyon took the lead and cautiously opened the door.

Much to their surprise, they were greeted with a purple curtain, which Tanyon swept to one side. Jakkon followed his elder's suit. "Incredible!" Jakkon breathed when he realized where he was—a throne room.

The throne room was not as large as Queen Aan's, but it made it all up in its decoration. The walls were covered with the same thick, dark-purple curtain that had been in their faces a minute ago. The floor of dark wood had a black-and-red carpet running down the middle of the room, leading to an imposing throne. Taller and wider than any other throne in Levea, the throne was a piece of art layered with plush pillows and coverings all crested with the Crakatonian insignia.

The floor was suddenly being shaken in a way that suggested footsteps, heavy footsteps. Tanyon pushed Jakkon behind the curtains and hide there. The footfalls came closer, and then they heard the sound of a door being opened. The elder warrior ventured a peek from behind the curtains.

A very large figure stood in the room with royal robes dragging behind him and a golden crown in his hand. He stood a few feet taller than any other man Tanyon had ever seen and was well-proportioned. Black hair was beginning to show signs of thinning, and his short beard that came to point just below his chin was graying ever so slightly. Another door opened behind the curtains, causing the two to jump, and a small, delicate girl appeared all flustered.

"Father, the troops are insubordinate! They will not listen to me, and they question your even existence!" the black-haired girl ejaculated with a stamp of her dainty boot. A husky chuckle reverberated lowly from the ample man.

"Dibla, dearest Dibla," he began in a soft pitch. "You get too flustered over such little matters." His voice was gentle in a betraying way. The modulation could place a person underneath its enchantment within minutes if the listener were not alert enough. Fortunately, Tanyon was anything but lax now.

The huge man continued. "The warriors will realize soon enough who their overseers are, and they will be subject. When I reveal myself, every man, woman, and child in Crakaton will bow to me. Then everyone in Levea will do so." An ominous chuckle followed the remark, and Dibla joined him. Soon the chuckles turned into raucous laughter that made the warriors shudder in fear.

"Father, when will you reveal yourself?" the teenage girl approached her father.

"Soon... Soon everyone will know the name of King Trea San III. Soon everyone shall bow before me and then before you." That statement began a whole lecture on the rise of the Sans.

Jakkon was horrified yet enthralled by the lecture, but Tanyon noticed something different. In Dibla's haste to explode on the king, she had inadvertently left her door open ever so slightly. With the cover of the curtains and the preoccupation of the dark royalty in their future plans, the pair could continue their rescue quest. Stealthily they inched toward the door beneath the curtains. Jakkon breathed a sigh of relief once they had reached the hall.

"Don't get too excited, Jak," Tanyon admonished. "We need to find Lordling Nic and soon…and won't you look? Six doors to look through first." Jakkon took the left, and the other claimed the right. "If you finish first, hold the hall."

∽

Jakkon Kingerly dashed to his first door and carefully opened the door to see that it was empty except for a few boxes which did not interest Jakkon. The next room was barren except for a crude table and chairs with a bottle and papers on the table. The glass vessel piqued Jakkon's interest for it was an exact replica of the one he saw men drinking from at the border.

Picking it up, he sniffed it. The drink smelled spicy and old; he tasted it out of a strange impulse. The liquid tasted like fire, and Jakkon reacted by throwing the glass across the room. The bottle crashed against the walls, shattering into fragments.

The warrior shook his head to clear the dizziness he felt from merely tasting the liquid. Once the unsteadiness passed, he took a closer look at the papers. His eyes widened as he flipped through them. *These are not any sort of papers. They are battle plans!*

∽

Nic was slumped in his chair, alone. He felt sore, exhausted, and starved. For several hours Burladase had been trying to extract information about Pneutra from him, but Nic refused to divulge anything. After an hour of just roughing him up, Burladase moved on to more bruising tactics. Nic's face had taken many solid punches during the past hour, yet he didn't say anything. Finally, Burladase was fed up with mere punches. He left to fetch himself a whip—an item that "never failed to deliver…" was how the general put it. Now Nicoron was waiting—painfully waiting for the inevitable.

The door creaked open, and Nic expected to see Burladase with a black whip in his head. Instead he saw someone quite different. "Who are you?" he asked weakly, not recognizing the young man. "Did Burladase send you for me?"

"No, I am Tanyon Fitherlew, a warrior of Pneutra, and I am here to rescue you, Lordling Nicoron Salindone."

Nic believed him to be bluffing. "How do I know you're speaking the truth?" Nicoron asked.

"Why would I not be?" Tanyon countered.

"How do you catch a unique rabbit?" Nic proposed a riddle. *Only a Pneutraite should know the answer.*

"You 'neak up on it," a slightly confused Tanyon replied.

The lordling was convinced. "Who sent you?" Nicoron asked as Tanyon examined his chains.

"I will explain later; now we have to free you."

"Burladase, captain of Crakaton, has the key. You will never get it from him," Tanyon smiled and left the room.

～

Jakkon was in the hall, holding their escape route. "Tanyon, I have to tell you something."

"Not now, Jak. I found the lording, but he is chained. Do you have anything that might free him?" The younger sheepishly admitted that he did and revealed two sticks of metal. One was straight and the other had an oddly shaped end.

"Put one in the wider part of the lock and hold it there. Stick the other in the lower part and move it around until it unlocks," Jakkon instructed.

Tanyon wanted to know how Jakkon would know this, but there was no time. He then disappeared into Nicoron's interrogation room and closed the door behind him.

Chapter Seventeen

KANEA AND TARI paced back and forth in the court of the jackrabbits, waiting for the two warriors to return from their mission.

"I am totally, completely bored out of my mind," Tari declared petulantly.

"I would think that after almost a week of nonstop adventure, one would welcome boredom," Kanea responded.

"Not me, I suppose I could really get used to all this adventure." Tari struck a pose as she dramatically recited, "Lost in the middle of unknown territory, encountering danger at every turn, meeting legendary bunnies…"

Kanea laughed at her description. "I do not think that the jackrabbits would appreciate the fact that you called them 'bunnies.'" Both girls laughed.

Tari sighed. "Really I haven't had this much excitement and fun ever. I feel like I was born for this. Although," she inhaled and exhaled, "all of the dangerous undertaking we've been forced to accept is nothing compared to the pure joy of actually becoming friends with you, Tanyon, and Jakkon."

Kanea was taken aback by her words.

"I mean," Tari continued, "you are such a wonderful person.

You're so kind and thoughtful, and the way you talk to me…it is like we're equals."

"We are equal, Tari. Sometimes I wish that I could be better acquainted with more girls my age, but people around me hold to the hierarchy. But to me, that hierarchy does not make a difference. In fact, meeting you has been wonderful for me too. You are so funny and adventurous. You make me laugh when I feel like crying. You inspire me to do more adventurous activities. Tari, you have been an encouragement to me on this journey." The dukeling hugged the princess like she would embrace one of his sisters.

"You have helped me too. Many times, I have just wanted to cry because I miss my family so much, but you have helped keep my spirits up and encourage me as we ride."

"I never had a sibling, so I cannot really understand how it is to be away from your siblings," Kanea replied. "I can imagine that it is hard."

"It is but having someone like you around helps a lot," Tari said and hugged her again.

Kanea hugged her back and wondered what it was like to have a sister to hug and have fun with all the time. Suddenly, the two friends heard a weird cry.

"Snake invasion! Snake invasion!" A jackrabbit cried before scampering away from three, huge, snake-like creatures. They were a brilliant blue in color, but their most striking feature was their two heads.

"Wolf creatures, a screeching dragon, jackrabbits with antlers, and two-headed blue snakes! What next?" Tari exclaimed.

A jackrabbit called to them. "Let them not near thee! Poisonous they are!" Kanea whipped out her bow and an arrow.

"Shoot them!" she told Tari. Her arrow flew and hit one of the heads of a two-headed, blue snake. She expected it to fall, but instead the snake continued to advance dragging the wounded head. Kanea grimaced at the grotesque sight. Working together, the two girls made quick work of the intruders.

"Where did those things come from?" Tari inquired of a jackrabbit that crawled out of hiding.

"They doth invade our tunnels occasionally." He twitched his ears. "Thou art brave lasses to face them."

"We have been practicing," Tari quipped. They laughed.

"Now I shall get help to remove these distasteful creatures," the jackrabbit murmured.

~

It took a few minutes, but Tanyon finally unlocked the chains that strapped Nicoron to the chair. Nic rose but stumbled in his weakness. The warrior braced the lordling.

"I think I might need a tad bit of help." Nic admitted wryly.

"Well, I did not come all this way just to have you stumble everywhere. Do you know how to get out of here?"

"I think so," Nic replied when they hopped out of the cell. Jakkon was still holding the hallway as instructed.

"Should we go out the way we came?" he asked.

"No, King Trea San is probably still sitting on his throne. Lordling Nicoron will lead us." They looked to the nobling for guidance.

"The soldiers brought me up the stairs."

"So down the stairs would be the other way out," Tanyon figured.

"That's too risky!" Jakkon objected.

"When have you ever been worried about risk?" Tanyon countered.

"When our lives depended on it. What happens when we walk out there, and those Crakatonians see us. We will be lunch for the wolves!"

"Stop making me hungry!" Nicoron scolded, and the matter was resolved. They would go out the way Nicoron came in. The trio sneaked down the stairs. Jakkon went before them and spied out their path. They were fortunate that all of the soldiers in black had assembled on the east side of the fortress, waiting for their king to give them their first royal speech. The courtyard was empty.

"A gray, empty courtyard," Nic muttered, "is unnerving."

"I agree," Tanyon said. "I wonder where everyone is."

"I do not know," Nic replied. "Whatever the cause, it is good for us."

"Unless they are waiting to spring a trap on us," Jakkon added.

"Thank you for that very encouraging statement," Tanyon mumbled. The wind whistled through the training equipment, producing an eerie sound that sent chills up everyone's spine.

"Look the gate is open!" Jakkon pointed to the iron structure. The main gate was closed, but a small door at the far corner was wide open.

Tanyon smiled. "That is our highway out of here," he said as they started toward the threshold. With Nicoron's weakness to consider, their progress was slow, and the courtyard was vast. Jakkon was sent ahead to spy and soon returned with positive information.

"All the Crakatonians seem to be on the east side of the fortress. If we slip out the door and turn to the west, we should be able to escape without being noticed."

"Good, Jak," Tanyon commended him with a grin. "Nic, can you move a little faster?"

"I can do whatever I need to, especially if it means moving in the opposite direction of this place," Nicoron replied firmly.

"Then let's try to run." With the strong warrior at his side, Nic made the attempt. The door came closer with every second, escalating their hopes; and finally, they were there.

"Yes!" Nic whispered.

"Let's not celebrate yet. We've still to escape the pointy borders of this grassy excuse of a country," Jakkon said as he gazed around. *No one,* he thought, *this is good.*

"Now let's make a break for the west," Tanyon ordered.

"But isn't our temporary base east?" Jakkon countered.

"Yes, but the east is loaded with Crakatonian soldiers. We go west then circle back east."

"But how are we going to know when to turn back, Tanyon?" Jak inquired. "Your lodestone is gone."

Tanyon thought for a moment. "We hope we meet Antlre on the way."

"I desperately hope you have an authentic plan behind that one," Nic muttered. "Who is this Antlre anyway?"

"Trust me, you will never believe it until you see him…" Jakkon spoke up.

"Now we shall make a 'mad dash' to the edge of the grass." Tanyon grinned.

"Year four, lesson ninety-two of warrior training. I loved the 'mad dash'."

"Do not get carried away, warriors," Nicoron reminded.

"Sorry, are you ready?" Tanyon questioned.

"As ready as I will ever be."

"Then, ready, set, run!" he commanded and then sped off. Jakkon pulled ahead of the two and leaped for the forest. The other two arrived a few seconds later.

"I cannot believe it! We weren't spotted!" Nic exclaimed.

"Now, shall we continue?" asked Tanyon.

A shadow suddenly loomed over him, and Tanyon saw Nic's mouth drop. Jakkon smirked.

"Is Antlre standing behind me?" The eldest asked, and his fellow warrior nodded with a chuckle.

"A jackrabbit—" Nicoron began. "but they were legends—not reality…" Antlre lowered his ear.

"We *are* reality," the giant rabbit replied. "That is why I can stand before thee."

"I can see," Nic squeaked. Tanyon and Jakkon enjoyed a good round of laughter. Finally, they became serious, and Tanyon stated that they should return to the swamp.

"A swamp?" Nicoron queried. "We're going to a swamp?"

"Sure, where else would we go? After that we are going to burrow underneath the mountains," Jakkon said.

"I hope you're jesting."

"Actually, Jakkon Kingerly is not jesting," Tanyon informed his friend, and Nicoron groaned. "After all I have been through, this should be easy," the lordling muttered.

"Now, all aboard the Jackrabbit Chariot," Antlre exclaimed. Tanyon jumped on first and then aided Nicoron in climbing on. When all three were settled on Antlre's back, the jackrabbit bounded away.

∽

One Crakatonian sentry took a swig of his drink. He was the one warrior left to keep watch while everyone else was listening to King Trea San's speech.

"Better than hearing a tiresome speech," he muttered in boredom. He raised his bottle for another drink, and a streak of white in the distance caught his eye. "Jackrabbits do not often venture this close," he muttered to no one in particular. "Better send a couple Crak-wolves on him." He untied a couple of the wolves resting in the courtyard and started them on the hunt with a sharp whistle. They raced out the gate, following the scent of the jackrabbit.

∽

Tanyon heard a howl from behind them.

"Uh-oh, sounds like we have some Crak-wolves on our scent," Jakkon shouted.

"Hold on then!" Antlre suggested as he increased his speed. Jakkon, who was in the very back, chanced a look behind them and saw two of the beasts running behind them. *Now I really believe what Antlre said about these wolves loving a chase.*

"How are we going to lose them?" Nic asked.

"I do not know," Tanyon replied. "I am just trusting the jackrabbit."

Antlre continued to race on. The Crak-wolves paralleled them and began to edge closer. Nic gulped as he thought of the ferocity he had witnessed in these beasts. Their tongues were hanging out as if they were truly loving the epic chase. Tanyon looked up to see the disgusting green color of the swamp.

"The swamp is near!" he warned Nic. Jakkon noticed that the wolves were coming closer. Antlre ran straight for the swamp. When right on the distinct edge of the grass forest and the swamp, the jackrabbit leaped into the air and landed on the other side of a mucky pool. Antlre stopped and looked back. The Crak-wolves ran straight into the swamp and fell into the mucky pool. They yelped in surprise and floundered to the edge, slipping and sliding back. Jakkon laughed hard at the wolves' discomfiture.

"You were counting on that, weren't you, Antlre?" Tanyon asked.

"Indeed, they fall for it every time!" The king chuckled. From their new vantage point, they headed straight back to the entrance to the tunnels. Once back inside, Jakkon, Tanyon, and Nic were reunited with the princess and Tari.

"You made it!" Tari exclaimed.

"And with Nicoron too!" Kanea added.

"Your highness," Nicoron dismounted and bowed before the princess. "I regret that I had to come before you in such a state."

The princess laughed. "Same here."

"Hope you had fun," Tari said. "We sure did."

Tanyon raised an eyebrow. "What fun did you have?" he inquired.

"We fought some of those two-headed blue snakes," she responded.

"You encountered some?" Jakkon questioned.

"Indeed, but we can hold our own, can we not, Kanea?" Tari linked her arm through Kanea's.

Nic was taken aback by the familiarity that the dukeling showed with the princess. As the others began telling Nic all about the jackrabbits, Tanyon took the lead with Antlre. The two leaders discussed the events to follow.

"My companions and I need to return to our canton so that we can warn our monarchs of this upcoming war," Tanyon explained.

"I understand. Your horses will meet you at the court. Do you remember how to get there?"

"Yes."

Antlre leaped ahead to prepare their horses. With his four friends behind him, Tanyon led the way through the eerie tunnels and right to the court. Antlre was already waiting with Desert King, Midnight Star, Prince, and the filly. Tanyon and Nicoron mounted the King, and the others took their respective steeds. One of the legendary beasts had the door out of Crakaton open for them.

"Tell your chief that we very much appreciate your help," Tanyon told the jackrabbit, and the animal nodded.

"Since the stars are out, you will be leading, my fellow stargazing warrior," Tanyon motioned to Jakkon, who was very surprised but did not object. They rode through the forest as dusk turned into the pitch-black night. Jakkon and Tanyon switched places, and the younger led them. Jakkon stopped for a minute, trying to find Shadrious the sailor. He didn't take long, and soon the five were riding again.

Tari observed the sky with keen interest. Stars dotted the sky like diamonds on black velvet. "It's hard to believe that those dots in the sky are the ones leading us home."

"I know," Kanea replied. "They are beautiful."

Nicoron looked up and smiled. The stars were bright, and there were no clouds in the sky; it was his favorite sky. He then sighed, and his head fell forward on Tanyon's back.

"Lordling Nic, are you well?" Tanyon asked in concern.

"Just exhausted and sore."

"We will stop if you need to rest a while."

"Keep going," the lordling admonished. "The quicker we return, the better. Tanyon, do you know how my family fares?"

"Last I heard, they were worried about you, but I haven't been at the citadel for almost five days."

"What happened that you have been away for so long?"

"The day after you disappeared, Jakkon and I were commissioned to escort the princess to the last competition of 'Horsey Day.' When we were returning, those Crakaton wolves and a dragon attacked."

"Must have been the Screecher," Nicoron observed.

"Well, it had a blood-curdling yelp," Tanyon replied.

"The Screecher is Dibla's pet and her ride."

"The Crakatonian princess?"

"Indeed, how did you know?" Nicoron inquired, and Tanyon relayed his adventure with Jakkon. Nic then told his side of the story. The girls jumped into the conversation and told their perspectives. The rest of their journey was uneventful, and all five were very grateful for the peace. Even Tari, the most adventurous of them, thought that the past few days brought more than she had asked.

Later that night, Tanyon observed that their journey was wearying the already exhausted lordling. He declared they stop and refused to listen to Nicoron's objections.

"You need to rest," Tanyon insisted and was backed up by the girls and Jakkon. So Nicoron succumbed to the others and later was glad he did. His fierce bruises ailed him and seemingly whatever touched him caused them to flare up in pain. Consequently, riding had been difficult, but Nic was willing to do whatever necessary to return home. A fire was started, and soon all except Tanyon were sitting around it, warming their hands.

"It surely has become chilly," Kanea noticed.

"It is fall now, Princess," Nicoron interjected.

Jakkon extracted something from his tunic.

"What is it this time, friend?" Tari asked.

"A flute," he informed her. "Would you happen to know how to play?"

"Of course, but wouldn't music alert our enemies?"

"We are far from Crakaton's border. Well, not very far, but we're definitely in Pneutra by now."

"Then some music will be good," Kanea said. "I actually read somewhere that music is something that takes away pain."

"I read that too, but it doesn't take away pain. It only takes your mind off the pain for a while," Jakkon clarified. "Now, Tari, do you know the Flather Tune?"

"Yes."

"Then play along, my dear little friend," Jakkon encouraged her, and she began playing a few introductory scores. When she began playing the main lines, Jakkon jumped in with a little song he had concocted.

> *The land of Crakaton is a strange, strange land,*
> *A land of wolves of monstrous size,*
> *And rabbits with paws alike my hands.*
> *Horses as tall as my knee roam the grasses there,*
> *With foxes coated in algae.*
> *Dragon swoop over the fields,*
> *With fire as hot as a kettle,*
> *And foxes to jackrabbit yield.*
> *Crakaton is a strange, strange land,*
> *The wolves which are the worst of it,*
> *But unto it, would I try my hand.*

The listeners in his party clapped. Jakkon bowed and then sat cross-legged on the ground.

"Jakkon, that was magnificent!" Kanea praised.

"It does need some work," he admitted.

"Indeed, it didn't flow very well," Tari commented.

"What can I say? I only made it up today."

"I thought it was very good," Nicoron added.

Tanyon leaned against a tree trunk, smiling as their friendly chatter continued. He gazed into the dark woods beyond, wondering if someone was watching them intensely—perhaps even a Crakatonian soldier. The flames cast flickering lights against his cheeks, and he stroked his chin. *This traveling with no sign of civilization is getting to me.* His beard was much longer than he would have ever let it grow—except when he did not have his shaving dagger.

Tanyon's mind wandered to his companions. Jakkon, whom he would have never chosen for a fellow, was now his best friend for they had been through much the past few days. All those years hiding underneath that mischievous outer shell was an intelligent mind just waiting to come out and show its brilliance. *How wrong I have been about him!*

Then there was Nicoron—a nobling and a warrior. They had never become very familiar with each other, but now there was a friendship between them. *How ironic,* he thought as he considered the fact that they both could get along so well after successfully managing his escape.

Princess Kanea was practically his employer, yet she was always the kind who didn't care for clan names or social classes. She loved everyone and never shunned a single person. *Every person who knows her loves her.* Tanyon could almost predict that her future reign would be one of the most successful reigns in the history of Pneutra.

Then there was Tari, and to say the truth, his first and final impressions did not differentiate much. His first impression had been that the young dukeling was no more than a reckless adventure seeker; his last impression was that she had become a more responsible adventure seeker.

His attention was diverted from his thoughts when Jakkon broke into another song to the Flather tune with Tari's fingering the notes on the flute. They laughed at the hilarious story told in the new song.

~

Burladase returned to the interrogation with his promised whip. "Well, well, little rat—" he began but failed to finish his sentence. All he saw in the mostly barren room was a chair and fallen chains.

Chapter Eighteen

ASHER SIGHED. NICORON had been gone for a week and Tari, Pneutra's princess, and her two guards had now been missing for six days. He was standing on the battlements overlooking the green forest just hoping that Nic would crawl out from under a bush or appear from somewhere, but for a week there had been nothing. *How can I lose my brother, my princess and my new friend in a few days' time?*

Denel came up from behind him. "Do not worry, Asher. Nic will appear sometime soon."

"You have said that for seven days, Den. I am beginning to believe he shall never come back." Asher's eyes filled with tears.

Denel dropped his head at seeing his friend's great distress. "I'm sorry, Ash. He was my friend, and I am hurting too."

"I know," Asher replied in a low voice. "I'm returning to my quarters." He turned to leave when he heard hooves tap against pavement.

"Asher, look!" Denel called to him. Asher rushed to the edge of the battlement. He let out a whoop.

⁓

Two days had passed since Nicoron's rescue, and finally they had reached their destination. Tanyon nearly yelled when he saw the turrets of Pneutra's citadel; however, Jakkon did cheer when they reached the outer gate. Nicoron looked up and waved feebly to his brother and his best friend. The gate was lifted, and the weary party rode in. Once inside, throngs of people gathered around them and cheered. Stable boys escorted their noble steeds to their respective stalls. The Salindones were summoned, and all cried when they saw Nic.

"Nic! Nic!" Asher kept repeating until he had his sibling in a bear hug. Nic groaned slightly but returned the hug. Denel was next. Then the lordling reached out to his mother and father who wrapped their arms around their son.

Queen Aan ran to her daughter and enveloped her with a warm embrace. "Oh, my darling!" the queen said as she looked at her long-lost daughter. "My, you are a mess!"

Kanea laughed at her mother's words and hugged her tightly, resting her head on her mother's shoulder.

Tari ran to her family and cried in her mother's arms.

"Tari, where have you been?" Reen asked as she held her tightly and rocked her child.

She truthfully replied, "Places that our imagination could never take us."

"Tari, never ever do that again," Kaete scolded her.

"As if I truly wanted to be chased by a Crak-wolf," Tari joked.

"A-a what?" Lura asked.

"I shall explain later," Tari told her.

Duke Runtron was last to be reunited with Tari. "My dear daughter," he began, "you need a bath."

Reen scolded her husband, "That is no way to treat your daughter who has been lost for six days!"

Tanyon clapped Jakkon on the back. "We did it, Jak."

"We did what?"

"Don't you know? We escorted the princess, a Teralian dukeling, and one of own lordlings safely back to Pneutra's capital."

"We did do that, didn't we, Tanyon?" Jakkon began grinning from ear to ear. "We're heroes!"

"The heroes of Pneutra!"

"More like the heroes of Levea," Jakkon clarified and produced the battle plans. Before Tanyon could say anything, Queen Aan came to thank them profusely.

"I cannot express my sincere gratitude. You saved my daughter. Tell me what I can do to reward you." Tears glistened in her eyes, threatening to spill over.

Jakkon opened his mouth to say something, but Tanyon spoke first. "Your majesty," he bowed. "It was an honor to escort our princess to safety, but we have something that requires your immediate attention. My colleague discovered battle plans from Crakaton."

"You went to Crak—Crakaton?" the queen stuttered.

"It is a long story, Mother." Kanea moved closer to her mother, slipping her arm around her waist. "I think you will need to sit down."

~

A few hours later the five teenagers and every noble in the citadel were gathered in the courtroom. Before the meeting,

Nic, Tari, Kanea, and the two warriors had taken nice, warm baths and had changed into clean clothes. Kanea loved the feeling of her lavender silk dress after having been in her cotton hunting uniform for six days straight. Tari loved the feel of being clean again. Nicoron, supported by Denel and Asher, simply enjoyed being with his family again. He had visited the healers and was prescribed rest and ice. Rest, however, would have to come later, because now each of the adventurers were to share their story.

Tanyon, who went last, finished telling the entire adventure from being chased by Crak-wolves to saving Nicoron and escaping the dangerous land. Every noble stood listening with mouths wide open, incredulous at what they were hearing.

The queen was the first to speak. "So, these battle plans that Kingerly came across, where are they?"

"Right here, your majesty." Jakkon produced the important documents. The queen passed them to her captain of the guard.

"I cannot read these! Jakkon, is this another prank?" The captain knew the boy well.

"No, sir. The documents are written in Feqar."

"What?"

"Feqar is the ancient language of Levea, but it was so difficult to write that someone created a much easier way to write," Jakkon explained.

The captain handed him the papers and said, "Then you can translate them as soon as possible."

Jakkon received the papers with a bow.

At the command of the queen, the five split up. Nicoron was taken to his quarters so he could rest. Tari accompanied her sisters to the archery field. Kanea went to her quarters. The two warriors followed the captain to the armory.

∼

Kanea walked into her room where the lovely scent of violets hit her. She admired the purple flowers that were on her dresser, probably ordered by her mother. She then made a beeline for her bed and, for the first time in almost a week, her body welcomed the luxurious down pillows with open arms. Soon the princess was sound asleep.

∼

Nicoron, aided by Asher, was confined to his bed.

"The healers said that you needed to rest, and rest you will," Asher declared decidedly.

"You don't need to tell me twice," Nic replied as he fell into the luxurious bed. Asher continued to talk away, telling Nic that he needed to rest as much as possible, but when he turned around, he saw that his older brother was already snoring. Asher smiled a little and slipped out of the room so that Nicoron could rest peacefully.

∼

Tari and her sisters wanted to have what they called 'sister rehabilitation time.' In other words, the sisters were going to shoot arrows.

"Who won the medal for the archery contest?" Tari questioned as they selected targets.

"No one," Lura replied. "The competitions never took place.

Once everyone realized that the princess and you were missing, the organizers canceled the games. Search parties were sent everywhere anyone could think of, but we never found you."

She let go of the arrow. It found its mark a little outside of the center bullseye.

"After that, everyone was afraid and running around like mad," Kaete added. "A lordling, a dukeling, a princess, and two warriors vanishing within two days caused lots of commotion."

"I can only imagine," Tari replied. "Did the organizers cancel the entire Nobling Duels?"

"I guess *cancel* wouldn't be the most appropriate word," Lura responded. "They more or less postponed them. The whole event was postponed so that they could have every available person out searching."

"And I suppose that it will be postponed for even longer," Kaete added. "You know—because of those battle plans in that ancient language. If Crakaton is planning a war for the near future, then there is no reason that the Nobling Duels will continue." Her sisters agreed.

"I know that if I were a king, I wouldn't be having fun contests when there was going to be a war," Tari stated. "That would be crazy."

"I agree," Lura added. "Now come! Let's talk about something more fun."

"Like Kaete and that Langhenian crossbow wielder?" A mischievous grin spread across Tari's face.

"Oh, I was thinking of you and that Asher Salindone!" Lura returned the grin.

"Lura! We are only friends."

"Right…" Kaete chimed in.

∼

Walking side by side, Tanyon and Jakkon headed to the warriors' quarters.

"Look! There are your boys, Tanyon." Jakkon pointed ahead at Training Unit 72 running toward them. One of the bulkier boys tackled Tanyon.

"Where have you been, Tanyon?" the boys wanted to know.

"It's a long story for another time." Tanyon stood and dusted himself off.

The trainees-of-war groaned and begged for him to tell the tale, but he stood firm.

"Young ones, your teacher is quite exhausted," Jakkon intervened and told the bunch. "I promise that we will tell you everything—later."

The trainees seemed satisfied with that answer, but they still insisted on following the two to the dormitories. Other friends came by and asked similar questions and were given the same answers. Finally, the duo found their bunks and could lay down. As soon as their heads hit their feather pillows, the newfound friends lapsed into unconsciousness.

∼

"I am so furious!" Dibla spoke through gritted teeth. "How could Burladase have allowed one little lordling to escape? He may forfeit his captaincy of the royal army of Crakaton. How could the prisoner escape under the guards' very noses? He was chained to a chair."

"My lady, I have not a single idea on how and why Burladase could have been so careless," a low-ranking soldier sighed.

"That is Captain Burladase to you, Sal," she spat. "No matter how careless he might be, Burladase still outranks you."

"Not for long," the soldier muttered under his breath.

"What was that?"

"I said nothing," he acquiesced. Dibla did not believe him but did not want to debate about whatever the comment was.

"The larger problem," he continued, "is what we are going to tell your father. We not only lost a lordling but also battle plans. That could be...problematic. I would hate to be the one to bring such unpleasant news to him." He gazed at the princess from under his heavy eyebrows.

After a moment of thought, the princess replied, "I do not plan to tell him." Dibla set her jaw. "If he flies into a rage, he might kill someone, and then we would lose soldiers we desperately need for our army. About the battle plans, I am not entirely convinced that Nicoron stole them. I think another idiot misplaced them."

"Sounds reasonable. There do seem be a lot of idiots around right now." The soldier nodded slowly. "But still, how could one chained nobling escape our interrogation room without someone seeing him? And then escape the country on top of that?"

Dibla turned and stared at him. "He could not have," she grunted. *Unless he were a magician.*

Chapter Nineteen

For an entire week, the citadel was in an uproar. Kanea was kept busy by making speeches and appealing to the lords and councilors of Pneutra for action. Tanyon, who always enjoyed a schedule, resumed mentoring Training Unit 72; Jakkon busied himself with the laborious task of translating the intricate battle plans. Tari and Nicoron were bombarded by questions from other noblings.

The major council of Pneutra consented to Queen Aan's request to invite all other royalty to an assembly to decide what to do about this upcoming threat. Each of the five were to give an account of the story; Jakkon would explain the translated battle documents.

Finally, the day arrived. Kanea dressed in a royal-blue gown with silver trimmings and a stunning silver cord for a belt. Carefully, she placed her lacy tiara in her dark-blond hair; she stood back to check herself in the mirror. The nervous princess did not want to appear like the girl she had looked like when they had returned from their excursion.

~

Jakkon and Tanyon dressed in the usual warrior suit. A long shirt, leggings, and leather boots along with the accompanying armor were complimented by their sheathed swords hanging from their belts.

"Jakkon, my friend," Tanyon addressed him, "you might want to consider having a haircut."

Jakkon looked at himself in the mirror and realized that in the chaos of the past weeks, his hair had grown to a length even unsuitable for him. Tanyon, on the other hand, had shaved and cut his hair to a length that made him unusually dashing.

A mischievous smile crept up Jakkon's cheeks. "If you will be my barber, then I will have my hair cut." Though he would not admit it, Tanyon was pleased that his friend was asking for a trim.

"Within ten minutes, I will have you looking like a decent warrior," the other warrior boasted as he sharpened his knife, and he held to his word. Exactly ten minutes later, Jakkon's hair was shorter than it had ever been, and much to his own surprise, he liked how he looked.

"Now I feel ready to be presented to kings!"

"Now I feel ready to be associated with you," Tanyon teased. "Come now, we need not be late; that would not look good for our image as warriors."

∼

Nicoron's knees were shaking. *Never before have I been in the presence of so many monarchs.*

Asher sat next to him and patted him on the back. "Tense brother?"

"Maybe, Ash," Nic replied meekly. He groaned, "Why do I have to be second? I would prefer to be last."

"I hear Jakkon is last," Asher stated.

"And why does *that* matter?" Nic asked

Asher shrugged. "I just thought you'd like to know, since he was a part of the team effort that saved your neck."

The doors flew open, and a servant marched forward to herald the arrival of King Andres Opalestene of Teral, King Fwerdin Werytil of Langhen, and King Zictor Videan of Dakiel. Each regal ruler took his place in the ornate chair designated for him. Queen Aan and Kanea followed the guests, then Tanyon and Jakkon, then Tari entered shortly thereafter.

"We have summoned you three kings here for a council to discuss a new threat that could destroy Levea," Aan announced to the other monarchs.

"What new threat?" King Werytil, who was in somewhat of a bad mood, asked. "You had better make this quick."

"Trust me, Fwerdin, this is important," Aan assured him. "Some of you may know as Andres does, that during the Nobling Duels, Nicoron Salindone mysteriously disappeared. The next day my daughter, two warriors, and Tari Helyanwe of Teral also disappeared. About a week later, they finally returned." She paused momentarily. "During their lost excursion, they discovered that King Trea San the Third, grandson of the King Trea San from history, is planning an attack on Levea."

"Another war?" Andres exclaimed. "Please, do continue."

"My daughter, Kanea, will relate her story," Aan motioned for Kanea to stand and speak.

The princess nervously bowed before the other rulers and quickly, but clearly, told her story. Nicoron was called next, then Tari, Tanyon, and finally Jakkon. Nicoron's story was the most diverse and caused much attention.

"How dare those Crakatonian scum kidnap one of our noblings?" King Werytil shouted. "And then treat him so rudely! It is unfathomable!"

Jakkon wanted so badly to say, "Well, fathom it because it happened!" But his manners prevented his outburst.

Andres Opalestene spoke next. "What about those battle plans? Where are they?"

"Here, your majesty," Jakkon stood with the translations at his seat. "They consist of battle strategies, numbers, different kinds of battle units, and most importantly, when and where they plan to attack first."

"Where is their first target?"

"Peasantshire, your majesty," Jakkon replied.

"That makes perfect sense," Zictor considered. "Peasantshire is the nearest village to Crakaton. Do you know when?"

"Two months and a week from yesterday, sire."

"That is cutting it close!" Fwerdin murmured. "We won't have time to prepare our armies. Armor and weapons are needed."

Zictor and Andres chuckled. "Fwerdin, we all know that you have your smiths make suits of armor out of feather iron. You have storcrooms full of suits of armor completed with swords," Zictor said with a laugh.

King Fwerdin glared at the others. "How would you know? You wouldn't have spies in my kingdom, would you?"

"No, but would you happen remember the tour you gave all

the kings at the beginning of your reign? You told all of us that you planned to make full suits of armor in case of a surprise war," King Videan replied. King Andres chuckled again.

Jakkon read some more of the translations until he came to a section named "Operation: Macula." *Interesting title,* he thought. As he continued to relay the information, the face of the ruler became more and more resolute. The operation was a plot to steal enough feather iron to construct suits of armor for an entire army of men, Crak-wolves, and dragons.

"Preposterous!" exclaimed King Werytil. "Carrying out that plan would mean an attack on Langhen."

"But why would they steal raw feather iron?" King Zictor questioned. "Why not just steal the suits of armor Fwerdin has in his storehouses?"

"Most likely, King Trea San doesn't know about King Werytil's stash," Jakkon stated. "Or he wants his own design," he added under his breath.

The kings and his friends smiled at the possibility.

"That must mean that I need to monitor my trades," Fwerdin observed. "There is a shipment of raw feather iron going from Three Gorges to Dakiel's citadel. Queen Aan, I would like to send a courier pigeon to cancel the transaction."

The queen agreed to his request.

Andres Opalestene spoke up again. "What do we do about this threat? Crakaton has planned an entire war, and I know that none of our cantons are ready for an attack of this magnitude."

Tanyon cleared his throat and stepped forward. "May I speak, your majesties?" he requested. Once he had received permission to speak, he continued, "I do not wish to boast, but since these battle plans have been discovered, I have been forming some possible strategies."

"Would they work?" Queen Aan asked.

"I have never been in war, but theoretically, yes."

"Tanyon was the highest in strategy class," Jakkon interjected, which was rather rude given his warrior class, but at the time, no one cared much about small misdeeds of the like.

"Please, continue," Aan encouraged.

"King Werytil, how many of these suits of feather iron do you have?"

"The exact number escapes me, but approximately fifteen hundred suits."

"That would not be enough for all of the armies, but it would cover some. We will have blacksmiths all over craft more suits and weapons from feather iron, and then use the leather and iron suits as backups. Would that be acceptable?" Tanyon asked, and the king nodded in agreement. "There we have basically solved our armor and weapon dilemma."

"What about strategy?" Fwerdin Werytil inquired.

"We have their battle plans, and they are very straightforward. What if we take control of their gate? It is the only way in or out of Crakaton—apart from the jackrabbit holes. If we take that, then the army will be blocked in. When they come to attack the pass, we can rotate troops and fire arrows and such down at them until we can diminish their troop numbers."

"What about the Crak-wolves?" Zictor Videan asked.

"I have an idea," Tanyon said. "We made friends with the

jackrabbits, and their king mentioned how much these Crak-wolves love to chase. Once the men riding these creatures enter the battle, we will have the jackrabbits get the attention of the Crak-wolves then bound off into the weeds. The Crak-wolves will definitely follow the decoys, thus diminishing their fighting force. Once the wolves are out of the way, I feel it would be safer to send down ground troops. With our four armies against their one, we will have the upper hand."

"This plan seems almost too simple," Andres observed.

Tanyon repeated himself. "As I said, I have never been in battle, but I do believe that even a simple plan like this will work."

"We need more layered plots and more surprises to spring," Opalestene said. "Crakatonians soldiers were known as the best in the land—better than even Langhenian warriors."

When Fwerdin Werytil cast a withering look at his fellow ruler, Opalstene snapped, "If Werytil is willing to distribute the suits of armor, we can have our strategists create tactics that we can count on."

Zictor stepped in. "Our armies can congregate in Pneutra, and—"

"Might you want to consult Queen Aan before you crowd her kingdom? She has already had to deal with a death and the Nobling Duels. Give her some time to think," Andres objected.

Queen Aan smiled graciously. "I will gladly take your warriors, as long as they are decent. If they're not, then I might as well have my warriors practice on those. Besides, it doesn't seem like we have much time."

The monarchs laughed at her candid reply.

"I know that Teralian warriors are very well-behaved," Andres assured the queen.

Tanyon and Jakkon slipped out. "Well done, Jak," Tanyon commented. "Your translations were perfect."

"Your strategies were excellent as well," Jakkon replied. They strode along the cobblestone paths toward the market.

Nicoron suddenly appeared behind them. "Hello, friends!" He clapped them both on the back. "I have the best idea that I have ever had."

"Lord Nicoron, what have we done to enjoy this pleasure?" Jakkon performed a mock bow.

"I am not a lord, Jakkon. Besides you saved my life and rescued me from the worst captors in the land. I consider the two of you my friends."

"That is very nice to hear, but I have heard from the general-in-arms that the queen is considering your initiation to lordship," Tanyon replied.

Nic scoffed. "I do not deserve her consideration. If anything, you two deserve a promotion. Don't you know why I was captured in the first place?"

"Yes, you have told us before," Jakkon stated. "A beautiful young lady met you after your duel. She batted her eyelashes, and you were in the bag."

Nic winced at his jesting words. "You didn't have to put it in such a blatant way, my friend."

Tanyon shook his head. "Nicoron, what was your idea?"

The lordling smiled. "Since we are all accomplished archers, I was just wondering which one of us is best."

"Are you proposing a competition?" Jakkon's eyes were twinkling. "Count me in!"

"Me as well," Tanyon agreed with a broad smile. "I think we all know who will be the best."

"Me, of course!" Jakkon boasted heartily.

"If I may remind you, I trained her majesty, Princess Kanea Ilindel, and that is the reason she is the exceptional archer she is today," Tanyon retorted.

"My fellows, my fellows, let us not debate on who is the best!" Nicoron admonished, "Instead, let us perform, and then we shall see, hah!"

∼

Kanea remained with the monarchs for diplomatic discussions. Messages would need to be sent, arrangements for foreign warriors would need to be made, and last and least, the remainder of the Nobling Duels needed to be completed. She saw nothing but tiring work ahead of her, and the lame humor of the four kings did not help lift her mood.

Queen Aan must have noticed the wearied look on Kanea's face. "Dear, I think you would enjoy practicing your archery," the queen suggested. The princess readily agreed, and quickly left the assembly. She quickly fetched her bow and quiver, then made her way to the archery range. On the way, she met Tari and her sisters.

"Kanea!" Tari greeted.

Kaete shot her younger sister a look of disapproval.

"It is fine for her to address me so, Kaete," Kanea assured her. "Your sister and I traveled the countryside of Pneutra for a whole week together, so she can skip the titles. In fact, you can all skip the title.

Lura was awed. "Really? Not even our princess permits us do that," she blurted.

Kaete gave her a wearied look.

"Maybe that is because King Andres doesn't have a princess. He's a bachelor, remember?" They all laughed together.

Kanea invited them to come shoot arrows with her, and the trio agreed.

When they arrived at the archery range, Lura pointed at the three older boys who were shooting. "Are those the boys who came in with you?" she asked.

"It is Tanyon, Nic, and Jak!" Tari exclaimed and called to the three young men. Nicoron rushed over.

"Could you four be judges?" he asked.

"Judges for what?" Kanea returned his question.

"We're trying to see which one of us is the best archer."

"Sure," the four chorused.

The three contestants readied their bows and shot.

Jakkon was chosen to be the winner. "I told you, I was the best," he boasted.

"Pride precedes destruction," Nicoron cautioned. "Trust me, I should know."

"Yes, as I said earlier—" Jakkon was interrupted by Nic.

"We know what you said earlier, so there is no need to repeat it." Tanyon chuckled at the two.

The sound of heavy boots clunking on the cobblestone attracted their attention.

"Look, it is Ghagden Uytil!" Lura poked Kaete.

Kanea raised her brows. "You know him?"

"Only by name," Tari replied. "Kaete here somewhat admires the crossbow slinger." Her comment was rewarded with a glare from her sister.

"I have met him before." Kanea stated. "He is a bit of a puzzle. At first, one would think that he is arrogant, but then you realize that it is merely his accent."

"He has an accent?" Kaete's eyes were sparkling. "I want to hear it."

Lura muffled a laugh. Nicoron saw him approaching their group and greeted him. "Ghagden, it is somewhat of a surprise to see you here."

The Langhenian countling towered over the Pneutraite lordling. "Really? It is you that never really favored archery, yet you are here at an archery range."

Tari thought she could hear Kaete sigh. *Oh, brother,* she thought. *Now we are going to be stuck with my love-struck sister.*

Ghagden surveyed the group. "Is this your entourage?" he asked as a knowing smile playing about the corners of his mouth.

"My friends, Tanyon and Jakkon, warriors of our canton; Princess Kanea Ilindel; and Tari, Lura and Kaete, Teralian dukelings," Nicoron introduced them. "I see you travel alone."

"Indeed, my assistant is taking the day off. So, finally, some alone time." He paused…"Or so I had thought."

"Please do not allow us to interrupt your lonely shooting," Nicoron insisted.

"We'll just be around here being merry and making enough noise to wake up the whole citadel," Jakkon interjected.

The girls started giggling, but Tanyon gave him a look.

"What?" Jakkon defended himself. "It's just a jest."

At first Ghagden tried to keep a straight face, but instead he began laughing. "Actually, some company from my age group would be enjoyable," he finally admitted, then he addressed Jakkon. "Is that a crossbow in your hand?"

When Jakkon nodded, he asked, "Is that your weapon of choice?"

"Indeed, my father gave it to me."

Jakkon and Ghagden immediately began discussing anything and everything about the crossbow.

"There they go…" Tanyon said, "off into *Crossbow Dreamland.*"

"At least Kaete did not faint over Ghagden," Lura stated.

"Indeed, if she had, she might have embarrassed our whole family in name," Tari agreed.

Kanea chuckled softly. "You three never cease to make me laugh!"

Chapter Twenty

ANYON FOUND THE next few weeks passed like a whirl-wind. Caravans hauling feather-iron armor were escorted in by Langhenian warriors; companies of soldiers swept through the lands from Langhen, Dakiel, and Teral. Soon the Pneutraite warriors found it hard to cope with the myriad of foreign legions that seemed to swarm the town square and market. Occasionally, Jakkon, Tanyon and Nicoron found time to stroll the lamp-lit streets of the bazaar in the evening. Hunters brought in reports of Crak-wolves exploring the Pneutra-Crakaton boarder, much to the dismay and despair of the monarchs. An attempted robbery of feather iron was foiled by the soldiers of Langhen.

"They're pressing our borders!" Fwerdin Werytil exclaimed. "We need to act faster."

Kanea knew that everyone was acting with as much haste as possible. Warriors and noblings were required to train from first light to dusk; nobles from every canton sharpened their fighting skills along with the warriors and noblings. Blacksmiths and woodworkers were required to make catapults and giant crossbows, while other blacksmiths used feather iron to form swords and armor. Tanyon was temporarily promoted from training trainees-of-war to supervising warriors as they practiced; Jakkon practiced in Tanyon's unit.

～

Nic breathed a sigh of relief; the feeling of his royal guardian suit was refreshing after the days he had spent in captivity. The armor he had was stained black with his ranking etched on the front; a black cape flowed behind and hid the sheath of his new sword.

A new, unique style of carrying a sword had been introduced by Ghagden Uytil who wore his strapped to his back. The lordling had adopted Ghagden's style. Nicoron chuckled a bit and unconsciously twirled his twin-pointed spear in his fingers. The spear itself was completely steel with the ability to fold into a fork-like weapon, very deadly.

Nic glanced at his chum who was dressed similarly to himself, only Denel held a gigantic battle hammer in his hand, equally lethal. The feathery, metal helmet they each wore was quite intimidating, and donning the custom-built protection made him feel formidable.

～

Tari stood on the balcony of Kanea's suite, staring with a melancholy air about her.

The princess approached. "What is the matter, Tari?" Kanea asked. "I have never seen you so somber."

Tari remained silent for a moment. "I am just jealous," Tari admitted.

Kanea's eyebrows rose. "Of whom are you jealous?"

"I'm jealous of every warrior and boy nobling out there. She sighed audibly. "They get to train and fight in a war. They get the thrills of battle, and what do I do? I stay around the ladies of the court who shudder and whimper at the mere mention of battle. I can fight! I should be out there training for battle alongside Tanyon, Jak, and Nic. Why do I stand here stagnate?" Tari finished vehemently.

Kanea chuckled. "War is no place for ladies, Tari. Really, it is no place for anyone."

"What is that supposed to mean?" Tari retorted. "I have the courage and the skill of any man out there. I can do what they do, and I even have more zeal than they do. So why shouldn't I be training to fight?"

Kanea then realized that her friend was being serious. "Number one, you do not have the skill of any man out there. Many of the warriors out there are nearly two to three times your age. Number two, war is not an adventure. We took an adventure. We hunted animals; we killed those snakes. Ours was an adventure, but war is no adventure," Kanea responded gravely.

"How so?" Tari inquired. "Everybody tells of war stories that are exciting. I want to be part of the excitement."

"Those are stories," the princess responded. "Think realistically. War involves nations fighting each other. People die in battle. People kill others in battle. It is *no* adventure."

Tari still did not seem to want to understand.

Kanea continued, "Tari, could you kill someone?"

The dukeling was taken aback and could not answer the question. "I do not know," she finally acknowledged.

"I know that you could not," Kanea answered. "I see how you interact with your sisters, friends, and animals. I know that you could not kill someone."

"I suppose not," the younger, impetuous one mumbled indistinctly.

"Besides," Kanea added, "if we did not stay behind, who would there be left to be the last responders?"

Tari suddenly snapped to attention. "What do you mean?"

"Think…what if our first move is unsuccessful? What if Crakaton invades?" Kanea began. "If Crakaton invades, who would be left to defend us if every young warrior or warrioress was on the battlefield?"

"I never did think of that aspect," Tari mused and sighed. "I am sorry. I merely feel left out."

"I understand," Kanea soothed, though she honestly did not find being left out of war very understanding. "But let us allow the men to go to war."

"Of course, Kanea," Tari agreed.

After Kanea left, Tari thought long and hard about what Kanea had tried to explain.

Chapter Twenty-one

"**W**E WILL ARRANGE archers in the trees and soldiers on the ground—all forming a semicircle around the gate." Lord Nanook placed miniature soldier figurines on a map. The lords, counts, masters and dukes of Levea were debating on what strategy they should use on their conquest of the Crakatonian gate. Nicoron stood back, listening as his father explained his almost-perfect scheme. "Foot soldiers will rush the gate, then retreat to the cover of the trees in hopes of drawing out the warriors behind the barrier. The archers will pick off whoever comes in sight. We will continue this maneuver until they surrender."

Nods and grunts of understanding were heard from the other nobles in attendance. The plan had ultimately been derived from Tanyon's original strategy.

Nic looked around. The royal booth in the forest arena was the only place of peace in the entire building. Since warriors and nobles proclaimed themselves ready for their first offensive attack, the monarchs thought it best for them to move everything to the woodland arena.

"Nicoron!"

Nic snapped to attention as he realized his father was speaking to him. "Yes, sir?"

"How many men did you see at the gate?"

"Not many—four or five."

"Why would they keep so little guard posted there?" asked a noble Nic did not recognize or know.

"The entrance gate is impregnable, and its location is relatively unknown. Why waste troops on guarding it?" Nicoron inquired.

"If the gate truly is impregnable as you say, then why are we trying to take it?" the noble retorted.

"If we can take the gate," Nanook said, "we can trap the Crakatonian army inside. Just like Tanyon said, our holding that gate is vital if we are going to win this war."

"And if we attack first, maybe we will be fortunate enough to catch the enemy off guard and unready," Nic piped up.

"Then let me guess…if we do take this gate, we move onto the fortress?" Count Uytil asked.

"No, we wait for them to come to us," Lord Nanook replied. "The fortress on the inside is wedged between two volcanoes. Any amount of disturbance could agitate the lava flow."

"How do we know they'll come to us?" asked a master.

"Any astute man of war knows that this gate is a vantage point. They will definitely come for it." Nanook Salindone looked around. Many of the nobles were already persuaded that this was the best plan. "If we leave tomorrow, then we will reach the gate by the end of the week."

"Do you think we are ready?" Master Colodrung queried.

"We have every soldier in strong armor with reliable weapons, horses with armor for the cavalry, and plenty of ammunition. If we leave this week, then we will be able to beat the Crakatonian deadline by a week," Nanook explained.

"That is not by much; they might attack before the deadline," Duke Helyanwe pointed out.

"This is our only chance," Count Uytil stated. "Let us not worry about what might happen and act on what we have. We know that the Crakatonian attack date is not for a week and a few days; therefore, let us make our date tomorrow." The count whipped out a dagger and stabbed the calendar.

"Aye," responded a few eager warriors.

"Won't it take a few days to reach the gate?" one noble wondered aloud. "It took the princess and the two warriors four days to reach there."

"True, but they were not traveling in a straight line." Lord Nanook drew an approximate path of the four adventurers. "We will proceed in a straight line—right through the lake and slough." When he heard the sound of groans echo through the room, he added, "I know ours won't be the most pleasurable of trips, but the needed repairs to the bridge have been made, making it now passable."

"At least we won't have to wade through the muck," Ghagden murmured to Nic who heartily agreed.

Jakkon sheathed a second sword and then mounted Midnight Star. The sweet mare now looked like a formidable warhorse in her armor, but Jakkon loved to think that it was only the feather iron. Theirs was an estimated two-day ride to the gate with no rest in between. Captains and generals began ordering their warriors; soon every warrior and noble had filed out of the arena in their proper regiment.

∽

Tanyon admired his look in the feather-iron armor. *No wonder Ghagden loves this,* he thought as he looked at his reflection in his feather-iron sword. Tanyon made his way to the stable.

"Desert King," he greeted his steed, "how have you been?" The horse neighed in greeting.

"I cannot believe you named that horse—let alone like it," one warrior scoffed.

"Horses are gentle creatures with very delicate temperaments. Some horses just like freedom and are very high spirited. You need to know how to handle such horses," Tanyon replied. "Desert King is quite spirited."

"Very, very spirited," the other replied.

Right then a noble came in and ordered their regiment out of the stables. Desert King gladly accepted Tanyon on his back and complied with each of the warrior's commands. Thus began their ride to war.

Chapter Twenty-two

TWO MORNINGS LATER, Jakkon perched in the boughs of a tree. He glanced down and gulped. *If I fall, I will at least break a bone—not encouraging,* he thought. Jak looked about him and realized that the leaves that he had hoped would provide cover from enemy fire were thinning by the second. *We just had to pick autumn for a time of war.* He moaned inwardly, and to add to the mix of terror, Jakkon Kingerly had never once climbed a tree before today. *That is something I will never admit. They do say that war makes boys into men.*

Around him in other trees were additional archers, awaiting the appearance of Crakatonian soldiers. Below him, Tanyon and several thousand warriors awaited the signal of the nobles. It was silent, dead silent, except for the wind sailing through the hollow trees and sweeping up the dead leaves.

Suddenly, high-pitched war howls chased away the silence that had been in place. Warriors rushed from the woods like ants out of their nest. The war cries themselves were enough to lure the enemy onto the turrets; Jakkon raised his crossbow. Arrows flew to the gate, and the warriors below retreated to the cover of the woods. The whistles of the arrows and bolts were ear-deafening. The Crakatonian gatekeepers were taken down easily by the excellent Pneutraite archers. Warriors on the ground tried another charge and retreat, but no more Crakatonians made an appearance. After several tries, the nobles called for a halt. Jakkon descended from the tree.

"What has happened?" he asked one noble.

"I believe we have achieved our goal," the noble replied.

"How? That was barely a skirmish!" Tanyon walked next to Jakkon.

"If there were more soldiers, then we would see them spilling out of there," Lord Nanook declared.

"But there was only four," Nicoron said from behind. "Maybe they didn't anticipate our coming."

"Wouldn't that be a break!" Jakkon exclaimed as they fell back into their formation. Strong warriors tried and failed to break down the smaller door. Tanyon was one of them.

"How can we get this door opened?" Count Uytil grumbled after trying to smash the thing himself.

"I know someone who might be able to get it open," Tanyon offered.

"Then be quick and get the man!" Uytil ordered the soldier.

Within a few minutes, Tanyon returned with Jakkon.

"How can Skinny here break down the door?" the count laughed.

"He won't have to break it down," Tanyon informed the noble. Jakkon retrieved his tools and began working the lock until it opened.

"How do you know how to do that?" Lord Nanook approached the warrior with a stern look.

"It's a very complex skill that is very hard to procure," Jakkon replied and then walked back to his battalion. Tanyon did not laugh though he felt like it.

∽

"The scouts returned and confirmed that all inhabitants of the gate were killed by the archers," Nicoron reported to all of the nobles.

"Interesting," Lord Quariopel mused. "They definitely did not expect us, or else they would have put more soldiers in the gate."

"Well, that works for our benefit," Nanook said. "Now let's take this thing."

∽

That evening, Jakkon and Tanyon were sent to search for Antlre and the jackrabbits with instructions to arrange battle plans with them.

"Where do we head first?" asked Tanyon when they were outside the gate.

"Follow me," Jakkon instructed.

"Where are we going?"

"Remember that rock that led to the jackrabbit underground tunnel?" Tanyon nodded. "I was thinking about tapping on that rock the same way that Antlre did."

"Do you think it will open?"

"Yes…yes, I do."

"I hope you're right," Tanyon muttered.

After a silent fifteen minutes, they reached the stone. Jakkon hoisted himself onto it and hit it with his foot. Suddenly, the rock started to move. The boy hastily jumped off. They gazed into the darkness before walking down into the hole. The pair did not encounter anyone until they reach the council room. Jackrabbits stared at them and whispered to each other. Antlre emerged from a tunnel and approached the warriors.

"What can I do for ye?" Antlre inquired.

"We are waging a war against Crakaton," Jakkon began, "that is every other canton in Levea—not just the two of us." Antlre smiled at his correction. "Our leaders were worried about the Crak-wolves and how Crakaton might have the upper hand with those beasts."

"Indeed, they are fierce creatures," Antlre agreed.

"You said that they love a chase," Jakkon continued.

"And we witnessed that fact in our escape," Tanyon added.

"Yes," Antlre raised a brow.

"We were wondering if when the Crakatonian army attacks the gate if you could bring out some of your troops and distract the wolves. If you can distract every Crak-wolf, then we will have a better chance at defeating the enemy," Jakkon explained their every move and tactic; Antlre followed along with nods and grunts. When Jakkon was done, Tanyon asked if Antlre would agree to the plan.

∾

"Did King Antlre agree with the plans?" Lord Nanook desperately wanted to know.

"Yes," Jakkon replied with a triumphant flair in his voice. "Antlre agreed to bring troops and distract the Crak-wolves at the final battle."

"Perfect!" Duke Helyanwe clapped his hands together. "Now we wait for the army to come to us. How long do you think that will be?"

"Not long, I suspect," Uytil said. "It depends on how long it will take for the enemy to realize their men are dead, and we are ready for a war."

"What if it is too long?" Ghagden asked. "Will we attack their fort?"

"No, that would be too risky and foolhardy," Nanook pointed out. "We will wait until they come to us. The end."

∾

The next few days were devoted to setting the giant crossbows and catapults in strategical places. Lookouts were appointed to watch for any advancing enemies. Three days passed before there was any sign of the enemy. On the third day, every warrior heard a shout. Tanyon rushed to the turrets.

"Look, there!" A lookout pointed at a black line in the sky.

"It is the Screecher!" Tanyon exclaimed after he looked through an eyeglass. The dragon circled the gate several times before heading for the volcanoes. Its screech bothered the ears of all.

∾

Dibla scowled. After not hearing from the gatekeepers for several days, her father had sent her on her pet to reconnoiter. Now she knew why. She handed Screecher's reins to a soldier and hurried to her father's throne room.

"Father!" she cried as she flung open the door. "We have been attacked!"

Trea San whirled around. "What is that you say?" he demanded.

"We've been attacked! The armies of Levea have formed an alliance and have taken our gate. That is why we have not heard from the gatekeepers for days!"

The dark visage of the king was grave. "Assemble the warriors. We must attack tomorrow."

"Father, they won't listen to me anymore," the princess moaned which she promptly replaced with a wicked grin. "But if you backed me up, then they would definitely do whatever I tell them to do."

Trea San stroked his graying beard. "Let's go to the courtyard," he suggested. "I will talk sense into the ones who will listen and beat it into the ones who won't."

Everything was moving at the gate. The large weapons were manned consistently, in case of a surprise attack. Crakaton had put windlasses in the turret, now much to the benefit of the Levean warriors. Archers lined up around the turrets. Tanyon was among the ground warriors along with Nic and Ghagden; they awaited the signal for their entrance into battle. Jakkon was stationed with the archers. Now the army of warriors simply waited.

Chapter Twenty-three

NIGHT CAME AND went. Some slept, and others found no way to sleep. Adrenaline seemed to be pumping through them even though there was no real danger at the time. Tanyon heard a far-off horn, unlike their own.

"They're here!" he cried to his slumbering comrades-in-arms. The foot soldiers assembled at the gate. Archers lined up along the platforms. Jakkon gulped when he saw the opposition fully clothed in a black armor with savage and rugged weapons. The Crak-wolves were a drooling, snarling bunch, ferocious beyond doubt. Their fearless and relentless tyrant rode a huge Crak-wolf, and the two of them towered over every other warrior. A noise to which Jakkon was not accustomed became louder. He could only describe it as the beating of a thousand hearts or wings. He looked up and beheld twenty or so dragons like Screecher with Dibla in the lead.

"That's not going to be helpful," he muttered as fear filled his heart.

"Behold, men," King Trea San summoned the attention of every person present from his jet-black mount. "These so-called warriors are so cowardly that they do not even meet us on the ground. They hide behind the stone walls here."

As raucous laughter filled the void, Jakkon gulped again. Someone tapped him on the shoulder, and the crossbow wielder jumped. "Kingerly, are you ready to give the signal?" Lord Nanook asked. "Now would be an excellent time."

"Yes, my lord," Jakkon hastily replied. He felt for his horn attached to his belt, raised it to the sky, and blew one, long, hard bellow.

This sudden signal caught the laughing Crakatonians off guard, confusing even their steeds. Shrieks pierced the foliage, and so did the bravest of the jackrabbits. Twenty-seven of the Sons of the King stampeded through the army, killing some of the men and distracting every Crak-wolf.

"Split yeselves!" Antlre commanded, and every jackrabbit bounded in a different direction. The wolves bolted ignoring their rider's tugs and pulls to pursue their prey. Jakkon was glad to see that some of the footmen had been slain in the stampede. Lord Nanook smiled; now it was time to get real.

"Fire!" the esteemed lord ordered. Jakkon raised his weapon and began shooting.

~

"Release the ground battalion!" Count Uytil instructed. Tanyon's heart began to race as the barrier was lifted.

"Are you with me, men?" the count inquired.

"Yes!" every soldier chorused.

"Then, charge!" the count raced out to the enemy horde.

~

"Stop shooting! Our own are out there!" Nanook halted the fly of arrows for a moment. Jakkon carefully observed the charge. King Trea San III did not look pleased, but he did look confident. A screech rang down from above. The dragons that had been staying in the air were sweeping down in formation.

"Man the crossbows. Man the catapults!" Lord Nanook commanded.

"Aim for the dragons!" Jakkon shouted. "Try to take them out!"

∼

On the ground, Nicoron encountered something he had never thought he would have do—real, to-the-death combat. The Levean armies charged into the enemy's army with the force of mighty horses, but they were met with something different. Nicoron was near the front lines. He expected to be slain instantly by the wildly waving of swords; instead he found himself locked in a duel.

∼

Jakkon peeped down at the battle below. Instead of the usual historic chaos of men and metal, there were pairs of men fighting, like a dueling competition.

"What are they doing?" asked another archer. Jakkon began to understand.

"The Crakatonian soldiers are trained in dueling. So, when our armies charged, the enemy warriors chose someone to duel instead of chopping him down." *Interesting.*

"Jakkon, watch out!" the other called out, and Jak nearly missed being scorched by a dragon's fire. The archers huddled in the cover of the wall, but the dragon kept spouting flames. Fortunately, one of the windlasses took it out. Jakkon knew what needed to be done and instantly acted. "Men, aim and fire at the enemy on the ground."

"But we'd be endangering our own!" one protested.

"Let your aim be true! We cannot stand here idly while our fellows are risking their lives down there! Watch!" Jakkon raised his bow and aimed at one Crakatonian fighter who was about to slice the head off a fallen soldier. Zwip! His bolt stabbed the fighter in the neck.

Nicoron blocked and parried his enemy's strikes.

"You're good," he commented. "Ever try out for some games? I hear there are a lot of gamblers wanting someone just like you." Apparently, the distraction was not working. The Crakatonian began twisting his blade and himself, making his strikes harder to decipher. Suddenly, Nic's feet were swept from underneath him, and he thudded to the ground; his enemy had bested him! He panted when he realized his time might well be up. Zwip! A bolt stuck out of his enemy's neck. *Thank you, whoever!* He thought as he leaped to his feet. The war cry behind him caused Nic to turn just in time to block a fatal swipe; again, he was engaged in a ferocious duel.

Tanyon caught on to the game early. *Pick a dueler and duel to the end. Loser dies. Winner gets the chance to die by someone else's hand. Perfect!* He was grimly sarcastic. Luckily for him, he was the best dueler in his training unit, and it meant something because he had bested three men so far. He was doing better than some; he knew that from glancing around.

Jakkon counted the dragons in the sky. Eight remained. *Those gigantic weapons are excellent when handling those fiends,* he thought gratefully. Even though Dibla had tried hard to keep the riders of these beasts attacking, the windlasses and crossbows were enough to scare away any dragon. Nanook saw taking the dragons as a priority.

"Take them out!" he shouted to the commanders of the gigantic shooting weapons. "Aim and fire!" Jakkon saw the number dwindle, some by falling and others by deserting, until only Dibla and her easily maneuverable ride were the only ones left in the sky. He whooped with excitement. The Crakatonian princess realized her situation and retreated.

～

King Trea San looked around him in anger. They were losing scores of warriors. "Retreat!" he called. "Retreat to the Twins." He had been able to preserve his black Crak-wolf and pounded his way out of the fighting mob.

～

"Release the horses!" Master Colodrung demanded.

～

Tanyon cut down his foe again. When he heard neighs and the accompanying pounding of horses' hooves, he glanced back to see that their steeds had been released. "Finally!" he shouted.

Desert King needed no time to find him. Tanyon grabbed hold of the galloping steed's reins and swung himself into the saddle. Nicoron had found Thundersbane and galloped toward Tanyon.

"Dibla is escaping!" the lordling shouted. "We must capture her."

"Don't leave me out!" Jakkon joined them on Midnight. The three rode in pursuit of the princess. The other Levean warriors cut down the remaining enemy warriors and then pursued the king.

~

King Trea San entered his throne room.

"No!" he cried. "Not again! Why must we always fail?" He spoke of his family's uncanny knack of wanting power but never procuring it. "Why?" he screamed as he threw open the door to his balcony—the same balcony from which he had given his moving speech but weeks ago.

"My king!" called a man. Trea San turned to see that it was one of the dragon riders who had deserted the battle. "Come! We can escape!" the rider insisted.

"You traitor! I saw you abandon our fleet of dragons!" The king seized a knife and threw it at the man.

The rider jerked his reins and put the dragon in the way of the knife. A piercing yelp reverberated from the lengthy neck of the beast, and the flying lizard leaped into the air, breathing fire in agony. King Trea San listened to the shrieks of man and beast, watching as both dropped into one of the Twin volcanoes.

"Serves the traitor right," the barbaric king spat. He turned to walk to his throne room when he heard a low rumble that seemed to shake the foundation of his fort. He swirled around in his long, fur robe just in time to witness the first splash of lava. The falling of the dragon and rider into the crater had disturbed the formerly peaceful, fiery mounts, and now they began to voice their complaints in the form of spewing lava and smoke.

He screamed and raced into his throne chamber. He rushed to close the doors to his balcony, but the mere glass could not stop the heavy molten rock that spewed from the angry volcano's mouth. It flowed like water and was hot like a blacksmith's furnace. Screaming, he raced to the door and yanked on it. Pain seared his hand and ripped up his arm. The intense heat of the lava had quickly made the metal doorknob blistering hot. The flowing lava quickly filled the room. King Trea San screamed one last time.

~

Lord Nanook had relentlessly pursued the tyrant, but the black Crak-wolf which Trea San rode was too fast. Nevertheless, the chase continued with some of the faster riders in the lead. Suddenly an explosion shook the land of Levea.

Nanook slowed his mount and looked up at the Twins. He was horrified to see huge amounts of smoke billowing out of the volcano's opening, and lava streaming down its sides and into the fortress.

"King Trea San III is dead!" came a cry from the crowd. Cheers rang through the sky. Victory was theirs.

~

The princess had flown up into the mountains with Nic and his friends following close behind. Her goal was to make it through the narrow mountain pass, but her dragon could not pass through. Dibla realized she had a hard decision to make.

"Be free, my Screecher. Go now!" She commanded her beloved pet, and the scaly beast lifted off.

Nicoron caught sight of the princess. The saying goodbye to her beloved pet had taken valuable time. "I see her!" he informed the other two and spurred on Thundersbane.

"Nicoron, this path is too narrow. Our horses could easily slip and fall down this treacherous way," Tanyon warned.

At his word of caution, the trio dismounted and pursued their quarry on foot. Jakkon was the most agile of the three, so he was in the lead. Nicoron, motivated by anger and a hunger for justice, was second. Poor Tanyon lagged, not used to dodging the many stones.

Dibla raced at inhuman speed, but Jakkon never let her get out of his sight. The pass ended, and all that lay before them was a large stone ledge and a cliff.

"You cannot make it, Dibla!" Jakkon called out. "There's no way out for you!"

She glanced over the edge and shook her head, as if telling herself she couldn't do it. "You will not take me alive," Dibla shouted and plucked hidden daggers from her garment.

Jakkon unsheathed his sword, just to be ready. For a moment the two faced off, sizing up each other's skill, intently watching each other.

Dibla was the one to begin the duel, suddenly thrusting forward, stabbing for Jakkon's hand; he easily avoided the tip of her blade. Dibla's movements were smooth and swift, placing excellent jabs and thrusts, but Jakkon matched her skill with his sword, parrying some and dodging others. She stabbed for his neck. When Jakkon leaned backward to evade her quick jab, he lost his balance and fell on his back. Dibla knowingly smiled at his helplessness and advanced. The warrior knew he was completely vulnerable.

"No!" Nic cried, and the lordling loaded his bow.

Dibla saw his movement, drew back from Jakkon, and then stepped over the edge of the cliff.

Jakkon leaped to his feet to see if, by some small miracle, Dibla had survived the fall. A sudden force knocked him on his back again. He looked up. *Screecher? Carrying Dibla?*

Nic's mouth dropped open when he saw Screecher and Dibla…and other dragons unlike the ones he had ever seen before. Those like Screecher they had defeated in battle were long, thin, and spindly. These dragons were thick and strong with rippling muscles throughout their bodies; their necks were thicker and shorter than Screecher's. Their claws were like wide blades. At first, Jakkon was sure the dragons would attack him, but instead, Dibla led them away. "See you later!" she warned with a maniacal laugh.

She and her fifty-plus dragon riders rode out toward the blue ocean. The three warriors stood staring out into the endless blue, watching until the dragon army was mere specks.

"Where are they going?" Tanyon asked. "There is no land outside of Levea."

"Actually, we don't know that to be true, Tanyon," Jakkon replied.

"Wherever they're going, I hope they never come back," Nicoron spat.

"I do not know, Nic. She said that she would see us later," Jakkon reminded him.

"Very rarely do maniacal tyrants carry out their threats," Tanyon offered.

"Oh well, if they do return, I think it will far in the future," Nic snarled.

All three agreed, and turning around, they headed back to their fellow warriors.

Chapter Twenty-Four

"**V**ICTORY TASTES so good!" Lura exclaimed.

"Lu, that's your grape juice!"

The sisters laughed. Tari, Kaete, and Lura were enjoying the huge victory celebration that all the cantons observed at no other place than Pneutra.

Princess Kanea, wearing a flattering lavender dress, approached the sisters. "Hello, friends!" she greeted.

"My, Kanea, you look amazing!" Tari was awed.

"Well, let's hope Prince Dashel thinks so," Kanea replied.

Tari did not understand at first, but Kaete did. "You have your eyes on one Langhenian prince, don't you?" the elder sister probed.

"One cannot deny that he is the most handsome person in Langhen," the princess insisted.

"I wouldn't exactly say that Dash tops all," Kaete muttered.

"Oh, I forgot, you're in love with that dashing crossbow wielder," Kanea interrupted.

"It is hardly love!" Kaete blurted.

"Well, he is over there with Dashel. We could go talk to them if you would like," Kanea offered, and Kaete agreed.

Someone tapped Tari on the left shoulder, but when she

looked, no one was there. Then she felt a tap on her right. This unknown person kept her swinging her head left and right for a few turns.

"Asher!" She had a scolding tone in her voice, but that slight annoyance soon was gone when she saw him. Asher was dressed in the clothes that made him most handsome.

"Tari, nice to see you again, too."

Lura saw that both of her sisters were practically gone. "I am going to get some more juice," she said, "and I don't know why I am telling you because you are not listening to me."

Asher chuckled, but Tari was indeed not listening to her older sister. Instead Asher and Tari spent the rest of the evening talking nonstop.

∾

Tanyon, Nicoron, and Jakkon sat in a corner of the ballroom, drinking their juice and laughing.

"I wonder what that drink in that black bottle was?"

"What brought up that thought?" Tanyon wanted to know.

"Well, I tasted it when we were searching for Nic, and it was horrible. I just want to know what it was so if I am ever offered it, I know to say no," Jak explained.

"Well, I think we'll be able to find out what it was fairly soon," Nic said.

"Why?" Tanyon and Jakkon said simultaneously.

"Because I heard from my father that the cantons are going to take charge of Crakaton from now on."

"You mean that each canton is going to rule over Crakaton at the same time?"

"Yes," Nic answered Jakkon's question.

"That sounds as if it would become troublesome," Tanyon thought aloud. "Four cantons ruling at once? Are they sure that this is the best course of action?"

"I suppose it is better than letting the Crakatonians on their own," Jakkon countered.

Nicoron spoke again. "I do not know how they will do it either but let the royalty and older nobility care for what they care for. I, for one, am not going to worry about it." He raised his glass and drank.

Tanyon hazarded a glance over at two young ladies who were eyeing them and started walking in their direction.

"Looks like you are getting your wish, Nic," Tanyon muttered.

"Indeed…" Nic ran his fingers through his hair then shook the dark-brown locks.

"What was that for?" Jakkon asked with a puzzled look.

"It makes me irresistible." Nicoron flashed a roguish grin.

Tanyon and Jakkon rolled their eyes. "Well, here they are."

The girls approached them bashfully. "Are you two Tanyon Fitherlew and Jakkon Kingerly?" one of them asked.

Nic was taken aback. Jakkon had to tell them the truth! Tanyon covered his eyes, trying to hide the way his face became beet-red. He had never had a smooth way when speaking to ladies. The maidens sighed audibly.

"Oh, we have been wanting to talk to the actual heroes of Levea for weeks," one said and giggled.

"Heroes of Levea?" Jakkon inquired.

"Indeed," the other replied. "Weren't you two part of the party who found a way to save Nicoron, and in the doing, steal those battle plans?"

"And you're Jakkon, the one who interpreted those plans!"

The giggly one had stars in her eyes. Jakkon glanced at Nic, whose mouth was wide open in disbelief and smiled his mischievous grin.

"Yes, I am the one who interpreted the plans. I would love to tell you more about it if you'd like." The girl's eyes were larger than archery targets.

"Oh, I would love to hear more about it."

Jakkon offered the girl his arm, and she looked into his eyes. "You have such pretty eyes," she coyly noted.

"I hear that a lot," Jak replied matter-of-factly, not truthfully.

"And your cheekbone structure is amazing! It's as if someone drew it."

"Now that is something I have never heard before," Jakkon responded, very much truthfully, as he grinned.

The girl took his arm.

"By the way, what is your name?" Jakkon asked.

Tanyon and Nic burst into laughter.

The other damsel cleared her throat, reminding Tanyon that she was waiting for his escort.

"Uh," he stuttered, "Would you like to hear *my* side of the story—from *me*?"

"I would love to!" she clasped his arm without even waiting for him to offer it.

Nic's mouth dropped open as Denel approached. "It seems like the hair and the smile didn't work this time," Denel cynically commented.

"Indeed."

"Not that it ever did, but—" Nic interrupted Denel's statement with a deathly glare.

∼

Queen Aan interrupted all the speaking.

"Please give me your attention for a few minutes," she pleaded. "Right now, the monarchs and I would like to award the five young people who were key instruments in the saving of our lovely cantons." She called Kanea, Tari, Nicoron, Tanyon, and Jakkon to the platform. She draped medals over the four Pneutraite heads and King Opalestene hung Tari's around her neck. The five young friends stood, rather petrified, in front of the hundreds of clapping and cheering people.

"I do not deserve this," Nicoron whispered, close to tears.

"You do deserve that medal, Nic," Tanyon ensured his friend.

"Indeed. Just think. If you hadn't been swept off your feet and kidnapped, we would have never saved you and then would have never found those battle plans," Jakkon reinforced Tanyon's statement.

Nic gave them a look that seemed to say, "Thank you, but again, no thank you."

The trio laughed together

"And exactly what is so funny?" Tari and Kanea were staring at them.

The three warriors refused to answer their question.

The two girls simply shrugged their shoulders at each other, knowing they would never be told.

But the honors were not yet finished. Queen Aan had merely paused for the audience to applaud.

"Lordling Nicoron," she began, "I do hereby give you your lordship for your fidelity in maintaining silence about our defenses even under torture." The Pneutraite crowd's cheers reverberated like a thunderstorm.

"Thank you, your majesty. You honor me." Nic bowed politely. "However, I do not believe myself to be worthy of lordship."

Jakkon could hear the astounded gasps and see the questioning looks on the faces of the onlookers.

The queen was taken aback by his reply. "And why do you think this way?" she inquired.

"I was prideful and allowed myself to be lured into a trap. A lord would never have permitted his ego to get in the way of his good sense," he explained humbly. "With all due respect, I must decline your offer."

The queen was touched by his admission, which only served to convince her even more that he well deserved his promotion. However, out of respect for his beliefs and honor, she withdrew the lordship.

"Tanyon Fitherlew," Queen Aan continued, "you are hereby promoted to captain."

Tanyon bowed and opened his mouth to thank her, but the queen was not yet finished.

"And, Tanyon Fitherlew, if you wish to continue in training Unit 72, you may."

"Thank you, my queen," he gratefully and graciously accepted this promotion.

"And Jakkon Kingerly," the queen smiled. "I hear that you have very much desired the quiet life of a scribe."

"Indeed, your majesty," Jakkon confirmed what she had heard.

"Despite the fact that this will be a very unusual action, I am going to allow you to change your occupation once you have fulfilled the four years of mandatory service as a warrior of the Pneutraite citadel. Meanwhile, you will start preparing for your apprenticeship as a scribe."

"Thank you very much, Queen Aan!" Jakkon thanked her profusely and bowed lower than the others.

The queen turned to her daughter. "Kanea," her voice quivered, "as you know, I must take the place of the king."

Tanyon glanced over and could see tears glistening in the Kanea's eyes.

"Therefore," the queen continued, "as I take the legal place of the king, you shall take my rightful place." Aan took off her signet ring and placed it on the middle finger of Kanea's right hand. "I will need you." Kanea nodded slightly, desperately trying to hold back the tears. After a quick embrace, the queen left the platform.

Tari began to doubt if she would be honored like her friends. *After all,* she reasoned, *what did I do to distinguish myself?*

She felt a nudge and looked at Kanea. The princess was grinning and nodded toward the stairs leading off the platform. Tari followed her gaze and saw King Andres walking up to the platform. With a grand smile and a royal strut, he approached the dukeling.

"Now I see that one of our young noblings from Teral has distinguished herself from among her peers."

"How did I do that?" Tari asked. "I did no great work besides killing a few snakes."

The king chuckled at her words.

"And not only did you kill them in the fiercest land of Crakaton, you faced the unknowns of that land with your other companions. Now I do believe that deserves an honor, but I am afraid that I have very little to offer you, except this…" He pulled from behind him a crown of braided vines.

Tari's eyes widened. "The wreathed crown?" she whispered in absolute shock.

Her companions were confused.

"What is the wreathed crown?" Nicoron inquired.

"Only the highest honor someone of youth could ever achieve," Andres replied. He held up the crown. "It is the symbol of courage, honor, and strength in our kingdom. Few dukelings have ever won it and never a young lady." He winked at Tari. "Therefore, without further ado, I proclaim Dukeling Tari Helyanwe the first, and for now, the only young lady to have received the wreathed crown."

The Teralians at the party howled wildly and chanted her name. Tari was astounded, not quite believing what had just happened. The others clapped and cheered with the rest, but they could never had truly understood the depth of achievement and honor this meant to the young dukeling.

"Congratulations, my friends," said the king, "and our great gratitude for your fidelity in protecting not only your own canton—but also our entire world."

Made in the USA
Lexington, KY
14 November 2019